# Universal Recipients

# Universal

ARSENAL
PULP PRESS

*Vancouver*

# Recipients

*fictions*

DANA BATH

ARSENAL PULP PRESS
103-1014 Homer Street
Vancouver, B.C.
Canada v6B 2w9
*arsenalpulp.com*

The publisher gratefully acknowledges the support of the Canada Council for the Arts and the British Columbia Arts Council for its publishing program, and the Government of Canada through the Book Publishing Industry Development Program for its publishing activities.

Book and cover design: Solo
Cover photograph: Roy Botterell/Getty Images
Printed and bound in Canada

This is a work of fiction. Any resemblance of characters to persons either living or deceased is purely coincidental.

NATIONAL LIBRARY OF CANADA
CATALOGUING IN PUBLICATION DATA:
  Bath, Dana, 1970 –
    Universal recipients / Dana Bath.

    ISBN 1-55152-142-3

    I. Title.
    PS8553.A829U54 2003    c813'.6    C2003-910382-X
    PR9199.4.B38U54 2003

for my mother and my father,
who have always told me that
writing is a good thing to do

# Universal Recipients

The Chinese character for "blood" looks like a corpse, seen from the head and shoulders, with a knife through its chest.

At various points along this serpentine mountain road, there are signs showing this *kanji* in white, glaring out from a lurid splash of red paint. I understand little Japanese, but the message is unmistakable.

somebody
died
here

Naoki once told me a story, after I told him that I am a ghost. He didn't believe me, and I don't believe his story, either. But the fact that somebody died isn't controversial.

Naoki explained that four years ago, at this villa I'm going to, an American woman got plastered on local *sake* and attempted a forward and backward flip over a third-floor balcony railing, with fatal results. I'm the first foreigner to visit the villa since then. Naoki has warned me that there will be tasteless jokes, and that people may hesitate to serve me alcohol.

He's also cautioned that the American woman's ghost wanders the house late at night and has been seen dying in various humiliating ways: drowning in the *ofuro*, for example, or plunging face-first through the glass doors of the fireplace. No one's ever seen her fall from a balcony. It's assumed that once she does, the hauntings will be over.

After two years, I haven't learned to like Japanese roads. They're skinny and hold too many surprises: missing guard rails, lanes that disappear, ninety-year-old blind truck drivers. Being a ghost doesn't make one unafraid of death.

My maternal grandmother died near the moment of my birth, in the next room. My mother informed me, as soon as I was old enough to understand, that I'm the ghost of her dead mother, and that my task in life is to right some of my grandmother's wrongs. This includes, it seems, providing my mother with some of the things my grandmother forgot.

Naoki's not yet there when I arrive. This makes me angry, and I'm unable to be polite to anyone. It's evident that this is a party of men, and that the women are wives who've been toted along to do the cooking, serving, and washing-up. One of them, a small, long-haired, retreating thing who looks fifteen, pours me half a tumbler of cold black tea. I turn my face to her blankly and, in measured Japanese syllables, request some beer. She stops in place, flickers an embarrassed smile, and glances at the woman next to her, a woman with short curls, big round glasses, and heavy limbs. This woman scurries to the styrofoam box filled with ice and water and pulls out a can of Asahi Dry. I nod, murmur *"Domo,"* and slip out to the log balcony, where the men are stretching their legs around the barbecue, toasting slices of marbled beef and curlicues of squid. The bespectacled woman scurries after me with a glass for my beer, then disappears inside again.

The men scuffle to their feet   *"Irasshai! Dozo, dozo!"* – and push me into a chair. They panic a little when I pick up a pair of disposable chopsticks, and laugh heartily when I decline their offer of a fork. We make our introductions and I'm unable to remember anyone's name for more than a minute, except one with a giggle and light freckles. Shimizu: he must be the youngest, maybe younger than me. I pluck a morsel of squid from the grill. It's undercooked and I chew slowly.

Naoki arrives and is greeted with great cheers and bows and slappings of the back. He looks at me sideways and gives me a slight, almost rude, bow. For the first time, I wonder if he invited me here only to be polite. Or if he's becoming afraid that, by being here, I will bring upon them some terrible misfortune.

After a lot of food, the men gesture broadly and insist to Naoki and me, *"Ofuro,* together, please, *dozo,* together." Naoki looks profoundly uncomfortable and tells me to go ahead.

After showering thoroughly, I step into the bath, gingerly, as it's far too hot. It's huge, as wide as I am long, and long enough for me to float from one end to the other, but only about two feet deep. You'd have to be very drunk to drown in here, I reflect. Certainly drunker than I am. After that first beer, no one offered me another. What would it be like, I wonder, to be a ghost, not because some dead person had felt entitled to my body, but because I'd been so stupid that I was embarrassed to stay dead?

I close my eyes. It would be rude to cool down the water, as I'm the first and it needs to stay hot for the others. Besides,

I've been told again and again that, after the initial sting, the heat melts the muscles.

I hear the door slide open. I keep my eyes closed for a delicious moment, imagining a woman coming to slip on the stone side of the tub and crack her head against a faucet, or to fall on the razor near the wall of mirrors and slide her thigh along it. I think that I'd like to have the company, for a few moments at least, of someone else who knows what it's like not to be real.

It's the little guy with the freckles, Shimizu. He looks sheepish, but he's been standing there for longer than he needed to.

"Hello," I say, sinking so the water touches my chin.

"Ah, *gomen nasai*," he gasps. He slips back out and closes the door.

⛩

Everyone has blood. All vertebrates do, and even worms and insects, although sometimes theirs is blue. My mother and I are both vertebrates and our blood is red like the blood on those road signs warning me that people die.

My mother says that when I was her mother, I often hit her until she bled. And that I once cursed her, saying that her children would make her suffer the way she made me suffer. That I'd make sure of that.

When I was in college and went to the psychiatric hospital and told them to lock me up, I called my mother and she laughed. She said she wished I'd done that long ago, instead of opening my legs and letting some man plant her inside me. They had to pull me off the phone before I tore it out of the wall.

I'm better now. I've learned that breaking one dish can do as much good as clawing up my face. But I'm learning something else: the further away you are, the harder it is to forget. I talk to my mother every day now: on the bus to my job in the mountain village school, or lying on the *tatami* floor in front of the TV, or in the staff room as I make myself yet another cup of instant coffee, or here in the bath. It seems I have so much to say, and I can finally say it because she's not listening. But I keep saying it over and over, because I want to get it absolutely right, so that when she does hear me, she'll know what I mean. And that means that I never forget. It was easier to do something else when I could hear her breath coming at me and when I could dream about somewhere she was not. Now I'm where she is not, and the dream is where she is. And I can't stop dreaming.

In Japan, a person's blood type is as important as their horoscope. My type, like my grandmother's, is AB. This makes us universal recipients, able to receive blood from anyone, but give only to each other. A person with AB blood has no immunity to other types. No matter what blood they're given, it becomes a part of them, and they never resist.

When I come out wrapped in a cotton *yukata* – I can never remember which way to fold it, right over left, or left over right; one way is correct for people who are alive, the other for those who are dead – Shimizu is sitting with a couple of the other men at the big low table near the fireplace. He jumps up, red-faced, while his friends roar and slap their legs. He bobs up and down in a ceaseless bow: "*Gomen, gomen, shitsurei shimashita.*"

When I insist coldly that it's fine, it's nothing, and turn to the nearest door, he follows me. Fortunately, it's not a closet; it reveals a staircase, and downstairs, lights are on and I can hear voices and sharp, rhythmic cracking sounds in various pitches.

In the basement, men and their wives are standing around with billiard cues. Two women are at the ping-pong table holding paddles, but when they see Shimizu and me, they scuttle over, shove the paddles and a ball at us saying "*Dozo, dozo,*" and then flit off upstairs, to clean something, I suppose. Shimizu and I look at one another.

Naoki is at the billiard table, and takes a shot that draws coos of admiration from the others. He looks up at me, and I'm suddenly afraid that I'll be asked to play pool. I nod at Shimizu and we go to the ping-pong table.

I'm not sure how I could hit anything hard enough to hurt anyone; I've never been much good at that sort of thing. But after we've been lazily batting the thing for a while, I feel, for a second, as though my arm isn't exactly my arm. I hear a different crack, and Shimizu cries "*Ite!*" Then he's looking at me with a kind of terror, whiter than I am, and a little trickle of something red and maybe steamy is moving slowly down his forehead. On the table in front of him is the ball, a bit collapsed, and cracked sharply down one side.

卍

One of the men takes me to our bedroom. "No balcony," the man points out boisterously and with a smirk. I give him the blankest look I can muster, and he continues to grin. "No balcony. No . . . sleepwalk, okay? This house very dangerous. Maybe you fall."

"Goodnight," I say firmly, and shut the door.

The bedding is still folded, and there are no sheets. I know where the sheets are: I saw boxes of them in the slipper cupboard when I changed my shoes at the front door. But I can't go down there again tonight. I unfold the *futon* and lie down, still in my *yukata*.

About thirty minutes pass, my mind as busily useless as a chicken in a cage, before I realize that I'm waiting for Naoki to come to bed, and that he may stay awake the entire night to avoid coming to this room. I don't understand why he is afraid to agree with his friends that we're together, but as the moments tick by and I hear various parting words and doors closing and the sounds of a house sighing with relief, I understand that Naoki has found some other place to lie down for the night.

I get out of bed and straighten my *yukata*. Perhaps he's still awake, I think, and he'll be different, now that no one is watching. I tiptoe out of my room, leaving my door open, and stand still in the hall for a while, wondering where one might go in this house if one were looking to be invisible. And looking forward and to my left, I see through the windows that one of the doors leads outside, and to a staircase that goes up.

Like a series of frames from a cartoon, I watch myself spiral up the steps, higher and higher, until it seems I must have passed the rooftop to trudge up through the sky. I finally reach the tiny balcony, which is balanced on a reed-like pole, and Naoki is leaning against the railing, gazing into the speckled lights of Yonago in the distance, like a brooding, boyish rock star. He looks at me, and then he turns his face away and stares into the trees below. He says, "I believe your story now. You must be a ghost. I feel like I can see straight through you all the time. You want me to be dead with you. Don't you?"

In the next frame, my hand reaches out, and it's true, I can see straight through it, even the bones. The only thing visible is the course of thick blue and red veins, throbbing. I start to feel hot with blood, this blood that doesn't mean life but only the possibility of death. One doesn't have to be alive to die. I could die again tonight.

I wake up with a start.

My door is open. From where I'm lying on the bed, I can see out to that window which shows me the staircase, each step a half-moon piece of log, going up. I don't imagine that anyone can come down that staircase.

I get up. My *yukata* is sticky now. I go out and open the door. I have forgotten my slippers; each step is cool and smooth on my feet.

The staircase doesn't go up very far, only one floor to the rooftop. There's a shape over on one side, leaning on the railing. Going toward it, I see that it isn't Naoki at all. It's Shimizu, starlight on his face, looking out toward the trees to where the lights of Yonago City rush toward us. He seems very small.

I go and stand closer to him than I need to. He glances at me, unsurprised, as if he'd called me and I'd come. He has a small, puffy mark on his forehead. He says something quiet and gruff in Japanese. I nod and we stand there together, our feet on wood.

Then I feel his hand, barely, touching my buttock. I shift away slightly, but the hand bears down, first only firm, then clutching me. It forces my groin against his hip, while the other hand grabs at the front of my *yukata*, hauling it open under the knotted belt. I start a scream, but the moving hand darts up and clamps over my mouth, while the other jams me against him.

I plant my hands against his chest. He looks small enough to crack in two, but instead, he stands, a solid, thin, concrete pole, while I push myself in an arc, backward over the log that holds me away from the trees.

For a long moment I examine us in my mind's eye as if we were a snapshot, dim and underexposed but still two clear outlines under the sky. And I think, deliberately and for what seems to be a long time, about the stories people tell because an awful fiction is safer than the truth. If, for example, a woman throws herself from a balcony in a drunken stupor, this is a sad thing, but it's over. Sometimes the best story is the one that's completely finished.

But sometimes we can't bear for something to be finished because we're trapped inside it, and so we have to make up a story that goes on and on. I wonder, hanging over this balcony, if I've been rehearsing all these years in order to tell my mother those words. And if she'll understand what I mean when I say them.

If I push hard enough to propel myself into those trees, will I stay dead this time? What stories will be told? To Naoki, for example. Will he believe them when he wouldn't believe the things I told him?

Thinking of Naoki I realize that all night I haven't been angry that he's been looking right through me, that he's been pretending not to see even my veins, which I know are real. As I'm hanging, the stars and the lights of Yonago pull the tide of blood up in me. My leg, for a moment, seems not to be my own.

Shimizu doubles over so suddenly that, freed, I almost do fall down into the waiting trees.

My grandmother and I have AB type blood, in both life and death. This makes us universal recipients, but we can give only to each other. If I hadn't been born that night, my grandmother might have had nowhere to go. But if someone else had died in the next room, I would have been born waiting for them.

As I get into my car, still in my *yukata*, still in the dark, throwing my belongings onto the seat beside me, I look up at the villa, a pile of pretty polished logs with big, dark windows like dead eyes. I can see shadows moving on the rooftop balcony: birds maybe, or ghosts, or Shimizu standing up out of his agony. I sit for a moment, listening to my blood quiet down.

I wait for a shape to plummet out of the darkness toward the ground, for it to be finished. But it doesn't happen. I wonder if she's so tired that she's started to believe the things people say, if she's resigned herself. Because in the end, if you're dead or not yet born, there's nothing you can do about the stories people tell.

# Bottle
# Episode

I kiss Joe's sleeping face and he reaches a sleepy hand up to feel my forehead. Then he murmurs, "You have to tell her today, babe."

I slip out of the hotel to take the SkyTrain to Waterfront Station, where my mother and my mother's girlfriend are waiting for me in front of a yellow half-schoolbus. As soon as I see them I have a seizure of regret, thinking of Joe still asleep, long and heavy and warm in the crumpled sheets, while I'm out here with all the anger and cold and damp in the world. The sky hangs close and grey. Pat and Addie, outfitted in warm green and black, are stiff little chesspiece figures against the yellow side of the bus.

As we stand waiting for someone to tell us what to do, I light a cigarette. Pat says nothing, which is admirable. A ragged man leaning against the building near them is watching me, and I give him a nod. He puts his fingers to his lips and pulls them away again in a smoking gesture. I nod again, and hold the pack out toward him; he trots over and takes two.

"What's your name, honey?" he asks.

"Lisa. And yours?"

He shakes his head. "Got a light?"

I've put my lighter back in my bag, and can't seem to find it. He holds out his hand for my cigarette, and I give it to him. He lights his own from it, hands it back to me, bows his head in thanks, and shuffles away down the street. I'm about to put the cigarette back to my lips, but Pat plucks it from my fingers and tosses it to the ground.

"Do you know," she said, "that forty-six percent of people don't wash their hands after going to the bathroom?" Her expression of horror is so sincere that I let it go, and don't light another. I have to stop smoking in any case, and soon. Now. If Joe were here he'd be lecturing, loudly, occasionally swallowing a quiver of tears at the back of his throat.

Last time I came to Vancouver to visit Pat, I took an afternoon to walk alone down to Granville and Howe to meet a friend. I turned onto Pender from Main and a man came out of an alley and followed me. It was the middle of the day, but I looked over my shoulder anyhow, and he said, "Don't be afraid of me, dear, I'm not going to hurt you." He had beautiful straight coffee-brown hair almost down to his waist, no shirt or shoes, eyes like black pinwheels. He walked me fourteen blocks and told me about dealing junk, about his ex-wife and his children he hadn't seen for twelve years. He told me about his client the social worker, who shot up in the company bathroom between appointments. "I told him," the man said, "that he's living a lie, saying to people they have to give it up when he's fucked up himself all the time. Excuse the language, miss. A lie like that will eat up your soul. You have to be true; you have to have principles. I don't deal to kids, and I don't deal to anyone who deals to kids. I give money to people who have less than me." He stopped, bent down, plucked something from the sidewalk. He held it on the flat of his hand, and I saw that it was a syringe. He put it in his pocket. "I don't expect anything from anyone that I don't expect from myself," he said.

When we got to Granville, I said, "Well, I have to turn here." And he said, "It was very nice talking to you, miss," and when I looked back he was waiting for the light to change, standing straight, shirtless, his long hair ruffling.

When I got back to Pat's place that evening and told the story, Pat said, "I wonder why he chose you."

Pat and Addie take a seat together; I take the empty one behind them. A tall white bony man with a shaved white head stumbles on with a fat pack like a pillow on his back. He pulls the pack off and falls into the seat next to me, stuffing the bag between his knees like a cork. "Greetings, friend," he says. "My name is Warren. Pleased to meet you." He lays his head against the back of the seat, closes his eyes, and falls asleep.

I watch Vancouver turn into trees, big shadowy prickly trees, starting sparse but then thickening by the thousands, climbing up the rockside hills and drooping under the weight of the damp sky. The guides stand up and introduce themselves, explain a little about the surrounding landscape: Douglas fir, lava canyons, waterfalls, the Coast Mountains, and the Howe Sound fjord. I watch the trees.

When I was a baby and colicky at night, Pat would put me in the car and drive me around until I fell asleep. It never took more than a few minutes.

Addie turns around to offer me a piece of fruit log. She is barely older than me, and looks a bit like me. People sometimes point this out before realizing how inappropriate it is to say such a thing. A lock of Addie's short blonde hair is sticking out to one side, and there's a smudge down the middle of one lens of her glasses. I try to break off a piece of the log, but it's rubbery and sprays coconut, and in twisting my morsel free I manage to fire it into the face of one of the passengers across the aisle. Warren, next to me, wakes up with a start, his bald head jerking forward. Addie is nonplussed for a moment, and then holds out the fruit log to him. "Much obliged," says Warren, breaking off a generous piece and popping it into his mouth. "And who are you ladies and where are you from?"

Addie and I introduce ourselves. Pat doesn't turn around. "Enchantay, enchantay," says Warren, chewing his fruit log and spraying a little spit. "I am from Spokane myself, but have been living in Japan for many years now." He pauses. Addie and I nod. "I am a Butoh dancer," he pronounces. He pauses again.

"I see," I say.

"Do you know what a Butoh dancer is?" A scrap of pink fruit log is clinging to his lip.

"Yes," I say. Addie nods as well.

"Ah. Well, good for you. And what do you do?"

The back of my neck grows cold and hot. My hand moves up to feel the nodes under my jaw, but I push it back into my lap.

"I'm a caterer," Addie says. "And I import European antiques and refinish them and sell them to the wealthy at exorbitant prices."

I stare at her. When Warren looks away to wipe his mouth with the back of his big bony hand, Addie winks at me. Pat turns to look at Addie with sudden interest.

I grin and say, "I'm in law school, but what I really want is to be a scuba-diving instructor. I'm thinking of making a career change before it's too late."

Pat's eyes, large and jealous hazel, peer at me over the back of the seat. She looks at Addie, and then back at me again. "Children," she says, "stop your silly games."

꿋

We pause in Squamish for a pee break. In the gas station toilet, I vomit three times, thinly and biliously. I watch my face in the dark, smudged mirror as I wipe my mouth, then watch my mouth forming one set of words and then another. The rims of my eyes are so dark and pained that anything my mouth could say seems redundant.

I call Joe. When he answers the phone, his mouth is full and he swallows. "What's up?" he shouts. "Is everything okay? Has your mother convinced you to leave me?"

"My mother isn't talking much. I can't tell if it's because I've pissed her off or because she feels guilty about not inviting you."

"Does she not want to meet me, or do you not want her to meet me?"

I look out at the parking lot where Pat and Addie are huddled over cups of coffee. Warren is standing with them, gesticulating toward the sky, the filling station, the pavement. Addie nods and asks him a question, her blonde eyebrows drawing together under her glasses. Pat's face is a blank.

When I told Pat about Joe, over dinner at a Japanese restaurant when I arrived last week, I told her that he was abrasive, and loud, and large. "On the surface," I said. I cursed myself for making excuses, but it's important to prepare Pat for things. "You can't imagine, Mom, how he loves me," I said.

"And how do you love him?" Pat asked.

"As I've never loved anyone before."

"Hmmm." Pat peered into the dish of sashimi as though she might be able to read someone's future there. "But that's how we always love, isn't it." Then she looked up and said, "You've lost a lot of weight, haven't you, baby? You look great."

And even then, I didn't say a thing. When Joe shouted at me later, I told him, "One thing at a time." Weakly.

"Hello?" Joe barks through the phone.

"I don't know," I say, shrugging although he can't see. "I'm afraid you'll hate each other."

"How could she hate me? I'm so utterly charming."

"You'll be with her for five minutes before you're yelling good-naturedly about white-haired dykes and the lesbian separatist agenda, and she'll turn into a hissing harpy. I have to get back to the bus. I'm sitting next to a Butoh dancer from Spokane named Warren."

Joe bursts into a guffaw. "That is priceless. What the hell is a *Butoh* dancer?"

In the bus Addie and Pat break out the rice crackers and Warren is delighted that we have not only heard of rice crackers but eat them. He pulls a packet of photos out of his overstuffed backpack and hands them to me one by one, explaining their history and gesturing that I should pass them to the rest of the bus, who look bemused and uncertain as the photos begin drifting their way. Looking around, I think of something Joe once told me about the "bottle episode," an installment in a TV series when a number of people are caught together someplace, and no one new can enter, and no one there can leave.

"Here I am performing in Fukui. I forget the name of the theatre. And this is in Edinburgh, at the dance festival . . . oh, here's one, this is my favourite, it's in the Koraku-en garden in Okayama. I designed all the costumes myself. . . ." His bald head is almost touching my shoulder as he leans to point to the images I can already see. Several of the photos are blurred. Addie has turned mostly around in her seat and takes the pictures from me, nodding, and at Warren's gesticulatory insistence passes them to the people in the seat in front of us. Pat would no doubt be staring out the window, but Addie is by the window, so Pat has to make do with staring straight ahead.

"I'll show you when we get there," he says. "Have you ever seen Butoh?"

"Yes," I say.

"Well, you'll see. I've brought some costumes with me." He pats his fat pillow backpack, but then he stops short. He leans forward and peers into my eyes. "You have very beautiful blue eyes, my dear. In Japan you'd be a star with eyes like that, although many people would be afraid of you."

"Thank you," I say. Pat glances over her shoulder with a smirk, but Addie tilts her cropped blonde head to one side and looks from me to Warren thoughtfully. Warren smiles, his white face serene. I wonder if maybe he took some calming medication earlier and it's only just kicked in. Then I notice that his eyebrows have been shaved off.

"They are not happy eyes," he says. "In my experience, people with blue eyes so large and brilliant tend to have difficult secrets. And . . ." he looks down at the photos still in my hands and reaches to take them away from me, ". . . they tend to be extremely nearsighted. In different ways."

The old-growth forest in the Elaho, one of the guides explains as we stand on the logging road about to enter the Douglas Fir Loop, is part of a proposed national park which borders on Whistler, and which includes the Upper Elaho Valley, which is the largest ancient temperate forest left in the region. The tract includes cedars and Douglas fir that are, in some cases, more than a thousand years old. Logging companies have already encroached upon the area and tours like this are meant to stimulate awareness. If after this tour you feel concerned about the future of this unique and irreplaceable forest, we will give you some contact addresses. . . .

I stare up at the sky, which seems low and weighty enough to touch the tops of the enormous trees. I'm shivering; my forehead is damp. Pat, next to me, pulls a green sweater out of her backpack and hands it to me. I'm annoyed by this, but I put the sweater on. Then I look at her face. She is watching me, her mouth set hard enough to push creases of suspicion into her cheeks.

We head into the forest, one behind the other like a caravan. I move into the crowd at the head, knowing that Pat and Addie will stay behind to take their time. Warren is a couple of people behind me, and I can hear him announcing, "My goodness, I have never seen anything like this. Can you imagine, some of these trees have been here since . . . well, since before most anything that we know about! It simply boggles the brain. Lisa! Lisa, sweetheart, come back and look at this wonderful mushroom!"

I look behind me. I step off the path to let a couple of people pass, but it seems that everyone wants to look at the mushroom. It's as large as a honeydew melon, moist and fire-orange, almost pulsing. It looks like a sea creature. "Oh my lord, the beauties of the world are just endless!" declares Warren, his nose so close to the mushroom that it looks as though he might kiss it. The others try to move on, but I stay with Warren until he's ready to leave the mushroom behind. He fondles it a little with the very tips of his fingers, strokes it like a cat, coos. When he finally straightens up, he doesn't seem to notice that he's been blocking half the party, and he doesn't apologize.

He walks behind me, and for a while neither of us speak. Then he says, "I hope I didn't offend you, my dear, with that comment about the eyes. It's none of my business, of course, but I have a kind of gift, you see. I tend to know what people are like."

I laugh. "Really." I look over my shoulder at him. He's not laughing. His face is very smooth and white and serious. The lack of eyebrows gives him the look of an extraterrestrial creature surprised by the human condition. He has deep lines around the eyes and mouth; he might not be much older than forty, but he might be sixty. He has blue eyes, like mine, but his are a pale grey-blue brought out by a grey-and-blue bandanna he's tied around his bald head.

"You're a hard one, truth be told," he says. "Why don't you tell me a secret, and I'll take it from there. Tell me what you want out of this life."

The person ahead of me hoists himself over a large fallen tree. I pull myself up to sit on it and pause a moment, my legs dangling. I pluck at the bark of the tree, watch it leave bits of dead brown tree-skin in splinters on me. Warren waits, as does everyone behind him.

"I'm in love," I say. I give a little self-deprecating laugh. "I don't think I've ever really been in love before."

I pull myself over the log and continue along the path. It takes him a few seconds to catch up. There isn't really room for two abreast, but he tries to pull up alongside me, bumping me presumptuously in the process. "And how do you know you are this time?"

I shrug. I think I feel a spot of rain, but maybe it's the slight wind shaking moisture from the trees. The man ahead of me releases a cedar branch and it wallops me gently in the face. "I care about him more than I do about myself," I say. I push the branch forward and hold it until I feel Warren grasp it.

"That's the first answer I'd expect. What does it mean?" Warren is panting with the effort to stay beside me. The air feels thick and wet, cool but heavy. I shake myself a little. I almost say, Look, this isn't really what's on my mind. But I can't quite bring myself.

"If he left me, for his own happiness . . ." or safety, I think, ". . . I'd understand. I'd wish him well." I frown at my feet.

"Ah. But that hasn't happened." I shake my head. "And do you expect it will?"

Someone left me once. At first he didn't physically leave – he was still there in the house, rustling the newspaper and sweeping the kitchen and shutting me out of the study – but it was as clear as if he'd stuck a sign on his chest saying *Back in five minutes or when you've gone away.*

Not long after I'd decided to marry this man, he dropped by Pat's house to pick something up or drop something off, and Pat didn't invite him in. I wouldn't have known this – he never mentioned it – except that Pat brought it up the next time we talked. I didn't express any interest in the incident, but Pat explained nevertheless: "I don't feel I have to have a relationship with him just because of you. If we're going to connect, it has to be as two individuals. And I don't see that happening."

"Does he plan to marry you?" Warren asks. I stare at him. He grins. His teeth are crooked, and quite yellow. "Your love."

"If he does, he hasn't mentioned it." I sound more affronted than I intended to.

"I'd have him marry you, dear." He nods sagely, his blue eyes steadily on mine until he trips slightly on a tree root and falls a step behind.

I laugh. "I tried marriage. It's not much of a guarantee."

"No, it's not a guarantee." His voice is muffled, and I turn to find him struggling out of a cedar bush that has engulfed him. "Not a guarantee. It's a declaration, that's all."

I hold out a hand and he hoists himself free. "Have you married anyone?" I ask him.

"No." He brushes himself, but he's still looking at me as if nothing, not even death or serious injury by cedar, is more important than this conversation. I look ahead again and continue on my way, and he plods after me. "Not in the traditional sense." I hear him stop behind me and he lays a hand on my shoulder. "Lisa, dear, look at that."

Ahead of us on the path is a fallen tree. Its trunk is as big around as ten people lying together in a pile; it's stripped of bark, polished and grey as the sky. Warren pushes past me and goes to lay his hands on it.

## Bottle Episode

"This is it," he says. He drops his bulging backpack to the needles on the ground and shouts, "Everyone! Everyone, please gather round. I need your attention for a moment."

Warren leaps onto the log and throws his arms to the sky. Behind him, beyond the fallen tree, the guides have gathered in a little awkward clump, murmuring to one another and glancing at him uneasily. "Friends," Warren proclaims, "I would like to perform for you a dance in the Butoh tradition, in celebration of the marvelous corner of the earth which we have been given the privilege. . . ."

At my shoulder, Addie murmurs, "I wasn't aware that Butoh was a tradition. Wasn't it invented only twenty years ago?" I smile.

Warren jumps from the log, limbs splayed, and lands on the path catlike. "Ow," I hear; he holds up one hand, inspects the palm, plucks at it with a couple of fingers and then opens his backpack and with several grand flourishes pulls out a river of lime-green chiffon. He gathers it up in his arms and gestures with a flapping hand for me to come closer. He passes me the cloud of green fluff and it swallows me to the top of my head; I try to press it into a more manageable wad as he leaps onto the log again, kicks off his hiking shoes, pulls off his socks and the bandanna from his bald pate, and drops the whole load on top of me. He crouches and murmurs to me intently, "If you can find the end of the fabric – ah yes, there – please hand it to me and hold on just loosely. . . ." He pulls out a length, then begins to wrap himself, over shoulder and around waist and then the same again, turning like a gyroscope until he resembles a tall barrel-bellied elf with a stream of green hanging from either shoulder. The breeze picks up the chiffon and moves it behind him like lazy sails.

29

I look up. The sky, if possible, has moved closer, although maybe it's just the effect of the dark magnitude of trees. Then I feel a speck of rain, for sure this time.

Warren is being the wind. He skitters from one end of the log to the other, his arms outstretched like airplane wings, his chiffon billowing. He's making wind noises between his teeth. He extends one foot ahead of him and hops on the other the length of the log until he slips and lands hard on his backside, which inspires him to stretch his white face silently in a skull-like approximation of Munch's *The Scream*. His chiffon has tangled around one leg, so he takes an elaborate several minutes to untangle it, loop by green loop, still seated with his legs on either side of the enormous tree, and with each movement he spreads his whole body in paroxysms of welcoming joy. Then he stands and begins to creep the length of the log, stopping after each inch to balance and twist on one leg or the other, and raise his face to the crowd or to the sky, lips contorting, eyes alternately stretched and shut.

Addie whispers, "I think we are seeing a rather personal interpretation of the Butoh tradition." I almost burst into laughter.

Pat is standing near us. Her arms are folded, and she is smiling slightly with tight lips, her eyes on Warren. I watch her for a moment. Pat's face, under the white bristle of her hair, is long and almost grey in the cold mist of the rain. She looks small but sturdy, like one of the young cedar bushes dwarfed by the age-old trees.

"Mom," I say.

Pat turns her long grey-brown face my way, and my stomach knots. She's tired, I think. She's tired of bad news. *Oh my lord, the bad news of the world is just endless.* What if I live a long and happy life? What if there is never any reason for either of us to be afraid?

The night I was attacked on my way back from the

university, but managed to get away unscathed, I tumbled home, without crying and without collapsing, to that man who would leave me, and he sat with me until very late. He made me tea and we watched the television and finally, at about one in the morning, I said, "I want to call my mother."

"Why?" he asked.

I didn't answer. I tried to imagine what sort of answer he wanted.

"You're fine," he said. "There's no need to make her worry." He got up and emptied the teapot. I waited until he went to bed, and then I called Pat.

He left me not long after that. Most of the time, when I think of him, I think of that moment, and wonder if there was something to what he was saying.

I'm crying, I find. I sink onto a stump, and the few people standing near me are spreading away like steam fleeing a drop of hot oil. I can still hear Warren's chiffon rustling. I feel Pat's small body close beside me, and her arm around my shoulders. I heave, and vomit between my feet onto the forest carpet.

I was ashamed of tears as a child, but when I grew up, at the end of each bad love affair I found myself running back to Pat's house and staying there for days, lying under a duvet on the sofa and weeping and being comforted with back rubs and rum toddies. I often slept in Pat's bed with her, and sometimes we talked late into the night, sometimes cuddled like puppies. Thinking of it now makes my skin creep. In Pat's murmurs, "I told you so" was buried so deep that only I could ever have discerned it.

I wipe my face and look up. Pat is waiting; beyond her, Warren is throwing his arms and face up to the rain. Pat's eyes are not blue like mine; they're a dark hazel, but they're the same large round shape, although Pat's vision was perfect until several years ago, when her doctor told her she needed bifocals, and she laughed at him.

"There's something I need to tell you," I say.

The rain comes down like the sea. Warren, his costume sticking like lime juice, takes a bow.

# Aerugo

The day of Rosalia's father's funeral, a piece of the roof blew off the Greek Orthodox church near my house and crushed a couple of cars in the street. Early that morning, I played Scrabble on my computer and accidentally learned the word for the thin green film on copper.

Munroe and I took the bus out to Rivière-des-Prairies for the wake, but he started feeling sick so we got off and walked along Viau. Everyone stared, but Munroe was with me, so I wasn't afraid. Then the road became nothing but road for a while.

The room at the funeral parlour was bursting. Someone behind us whispered, "The daughter's not married yet, is she?" The smell of lilies everywhere and the body silent in the casket – I don't think I'd ever seen a dead body before – the family seated in a semicircle waiting for handshakes. I didn't go up; I didn't have anything to say to a dead man I'd never met.

Munroe's eyes chastized me; his life has been full of these rituals, things no one has ever given me the chance to see. I would have stayed all afternoon, smelling the flowers and watching the struggle for quiet on Rosalia's mother's face. But he made me go.

On the way home, Munroe and I walked past the Greek Orthodox church, the slice of roof like a shaving of chocolate curled up on the front steps. "The green that forms on copper is called aerugo," I told him. "I didn't even know copper turned green until I moved to Montreal."

"Me either," he said. "Small towns don't teach you much."

"But," I said, "I could have learned the word anywhere."

I dreamt about Rivière-des-Prairies every night for the rest of the week. Not about the still dead face and the still perfume of the lilies, but about the north end of Boulevard Viau, lined with trees and blank apartment buildings and then blocks of nothing, suddenly opening up onto a funeral home all alone, with no place nearby for anyone to die in.

# Begin and End Frequently

# I
# TOKYO

Everything is about context, and here there is none.

I meet Gregory in an elevator. Friends have left without me, and I'm about to tuck into my tears when a hand keeps the door open and in he comes. He crinkles at me, and I try, but I sense he can see all of me, patchy with hunger and fatigue.

He's going for dinner, and when he hears my story he invites me. This will mean a stranger, but everyone's a stranger here, and I really must eat.

Tokyo is a carnival, and I would have been too frightened to come out here alone. We rustle under Shinjuku, and he's talking at me, saying a lot of things I already know about cultural climates and not blowing your nose in the subway.

*So if I wanted to arouse you really slowly,*
*what would I do?*

39

*I'd probably hurt you. I might
knock you over and bruise you.*

*Maybe I'd have to tie you down.*

*I get impatient. Maybe it
makes me feel vulnerable.*

*I like to be in control.
I like to be the one giving.*

*Nothing would turn me on more
than to see you lie back, to explore you.
To see you vulnerable.*

*I might cry. Or something.*

This is a landscape. My first three-thousand-degree angle on it
is wrapped around him, and whenever I retrieve Tokyo from my
mind he'll be there. I know this already, although I don't think
I'll ever see him again. We find a cheap sushi shop, we each buy a
*bento*, we tumble iced coffee out of a vending machine, we sit on
the steps of the station because there's nowhere else to sit, and
we watch the people in cardboard houses and the people who
are reveling in the imperative places that are waiting for them.

The friends I missed earlier coil by in a train, and I feel
splendid and adventurous, here with this man I just met (who
might be a maniac, but) who has a long throat and smooth
temples muzzled in thick hair. The friends express surprise. I
introduce. They flicker away with promises, and Gregory and I
brush ourselves off.

I'm tired. This city is a big, noisy cartoon and right now it
means less to me than any city ever has. Everything that ripples
by seems delinquent, fraught, inlaid with danger. Not danger

like losing your wallet or being raped in an alleyway; more like a feral thing cooped inside one of those plastic balls from bubble-gum machines. This man is still telling me stories as if he knows where I need to go from here. The lights come down like needles and my skin is like the thinnest porcelain imaginable, so thin that rather than crack it will probably crumble. I want to go back to that big cool hotel which is so like a little America except that everybody bows incessantly. I want to get into bed and go to sleep, because sleep is a familiar place.

## II
## SHODOSHIMA

*Talk naughty to me.*

*I'm better at being naughty*
*than talking naughty.*

*You're very withheld most of the time.*

*I don't have the words for these things.*

*If I were there right now,*
*what would you do?*

*Whatever you wanted.*
*Why don't you tell me.*

Last night Gregory and I crashed together on a comforter and didn't speak. He fell asleep quickly; I didn't. Today he's sunburnt on his neck, schmoozing the *yakuza* with the teenage wife in the white bikini. Gregory wants to go waterskiing and is certain that the *yakuza* guy, glittering with medallions, will take him. Matthew has suggested that if Gregory stays in Japan for a couple of years he'll end up running a *pachinko* parlour and missing a little finger. This doesn't seem farfetched.

Matthew asked me this morning, as we were walking from the ferry, if I was okay. He and I lie down in the shade, the sand under us like burlap. Matthew's feet are resting on my lower back and his hat is over his face; I'm smoking and reading Fumiko Enchi (in translation).

I watch Gregory's back. The *yakuza* nods.

Later, when we start setting up the tents, Gregory is babbling to Matthew about his attempt to manoeuvre on one ski. He's still wet and panting, although he came in from the water over an hour ago. It's tacitly understood between Gregory and me that we'll share a tent. I'm not sure how this came about. I'm glad.

When we've finished setting up, Matthew mentions the rowboats, offering to row us to the closest island. Gregory looks ambivalent, and then says he'll stay behind.

The water's full of jellyfish, and I'm concerned that the rickety boat will capsize. I'm also concerned that I should be happy to be in the boat with Matthew. My shoulders are sore from the sun and my head's heavy; I'd really like a nap, or maybe a beer. I've barely eaten today; the combination of heat and discomfiture has made this easy.

On the island, we climb to the top of a mound of rock and sit to watch the last smudges of the sunset. I wonder if it's a good idea to be so far out when it's getting dark.

"This place is marvelous," Matthew says. I nod. We can see the shore of Shodoshima, still dotted with people in swimsuits. Japan pop music is whispering. The sea is thick, and not clean, but salty and wet nevertheless. Tonight we'll sleep on the beach. Somewhere over there, Gregory's chatting up some gangster or some beach babe. I'm so happy to be here that I'm confused.

On the way back, pinched in the airtight wringer of the sky and the water, and once we're thrown ashore like debris, crusty with salt, I feel as though my topsoil has all been scraped off. The water wasn't sweet, the beer coats my insides like enamel, and something in me has drifted. Gregory's there, looking like a pinkish crayon sketch of himself, under the gaslights. I wonder if we're on the cusp of something, or headed toward the core of something, but right now it all seems like too much effort. He sits as absorbent and watchful as a bloodhound, but not for me. There are multitudes of things more important than me at this moment.

I often cling to people like fetishes, even after they're proven cold-fisted or torn or simply unworthy.

Then he looks at me and says, "Let's go to sleep."

We climb into the smaller tent and I lie there draining. Savouring. He's nearby, after all. "Did you have a good time today?" I ask.

Gregory nods. "That guy is a useful person to know. I think tomorrow he might take me on his boat. He might invite you too, if you're nice to him a bit."

I don't reply. Outside, the cicadas and the frogs are shrieking at one another. We don't say anything for a little while, and the night grows cavernous, as though we aren't in a tent at all but staring up at a sky which has given up all its stars.

Gregory isn't pretty. I can't see him, but I remember. His face is all marked from adolescence; everything about him is skinny. I remember, though, that his eyes are almost black. And he and Matthew, together, are pretty, when they smack each other and when they don't, when they call each other names, or when Gregory talks about Matthew in the dark.

"What's the name of the first boy you ever kissed?" Gregory asks.

"Garry Rousseau. I was six."

"Jesus. Precocious."

"And you? What's the name of the first boy you ever kissed?"

He hesitates. "Brian Thierfelder."

I'm taken aback, and don't speak for a moment. I wonder if this pleases him. "And how old were you?" I ask finally.

"Ummmm . . . twenty-four? Twenty-five?"

We pause for a moment, and I feel him waiting. "Was it good?"

"Oh yes."

"Did you do more than kiss him?"

"Oh yes."

"Have there been others since then?"

"One other."

"Anyone I know?"

Pause. "No."

"Damn."

"What?"

"Nothing."

Silence. I want to reach over, but the night's getting larger.

"So, how often have you been touched since you arrived?" he asks.

I think. "Not often. Would you sleep with Matthew?" I ask.

"No. Would you?"

"I don't know. It would depend on what happened first."

His voice is quiet. "What would have to happen first?"

"He'd have to ask me a lot of questions."

Gregory curls up around me, pressing against my back. (Even in this heat.) I fall asleep quickly, although I know he won't.


# III
# OKAYAMA


On Sunday night I'm back in my little house, tingling all over and slapping at things in a fruitless release of energy.

Matthew calls. He's so near, and so much kinder. He asks me to come to dinner. I bring a melon. He makes fried rice with vegetables that are just a little too crunchy. There's lots of beer.

It only seems reasonable, what happens next.

## IV
## OSAKA

When I get my photographs back I realize that I was wrong. Gregory's tall and firm and has a hungry, crisp face, and even in the chocolate silhouettes I can see that his eyes are tender and sad. He's lovely. I wonder how I failed to see it before.

*First I'd undress.*

*Would you let me undress you?*

*Only if you promised to fuck me really hard.*

Now he tells me, as we're lying on his spindly futon on his *tatami* in Osaka, that at one time his eyes were cement-cold.

"They aren't any more," I say.

I'm willing, so willing I'm exhausted, and he's not, because he wants to preserve something that he won't explain to me. I feel as though I've lugged all my bruises to Osaka with me and they sit on my skin, embossed, the colour of blood, relentless. In the night, in between sleep, Gregory grips and wrestles me, moves over me like streams, then unexpectedly brakes and renounces and sleeps again. My brain, even in my dreams, is as thick as soot.

In the daylight we eat *zarusoba* and wander around DenDen Town, mostly in the rain. I feel as though we take up acres, but in this city even *guijin* are more or less unremarkable,

45

and we're jostled and swayed as easily as anyone else.

I stopped fumbling with continuity a long time ago. Now the elemental thing is to begin and end frequently and expressly, and never to be sorry. I fasten myself to people with hinges, not with bolts. I have enough surfaces for everyone.

One night he clings to me in his sleep and whimpers my name. "Bad dreams," he says. "Bad memories." I put myself around him and offer a few words, but he's asleep again.

## V

## KYOTO

Later, all I remember is climbing the hill hand in hand, and then releasing him to step to the periphery. The temple is behind me, with people, and above and below me is the hillside creaking with wind and dense trees, and then, far beyond, the contours of Kyoto, like a river of sign language, too bursting with meaning to be understood. I stand there and try to become something that will encompass this. I turn and he's behind me. When he sees my face, his becomes soft as a handful of grain. "Oh. Good." His voice has melted.

I say, "I can't believe this is my life."

*Do you think there's anyone else I can talk to?*

*I guess you're saying there isn't.*

*That's right.*

*I don't think there's anything in my life that I haven't told over and over.*

## Begin and End Frequently

*I don't believe in giving things away for free.*

*That makes me feel . . . privileged.*

*Well, you're welcome. I'm glad I met you.*
*A lot of things will come and go,*
*but I think you'll stay.*

*I wish you were here.*

*If I were, what would you do to me?*

*Anything you wanted.*

*Tell me.*

# A Kettle

Eliza is sitting on the end of her bed painting her toenails a colour called Toad. Jude stands in front of her looking out the window. She's trying to think of something to say.

"I'd better go," he says finally.

"No," she says, "stay for coffee at least. Or tea. Would you rather have tea?"

"He'll be home soon." Jude presses his fingertips against the window pane. "Do you paint your toenails every morning?"

She wants to look down for the rest of the day, once he's gone, and see a colour she doesn't expect. "He won't mind," she says. "There's nothing for him to mind. Come on, I have bagels. Unless you need to go for some other reason."

"No. I feel strange."

Eliza pushes the brush back into the bottle and screws it on tight. She stretches her legs out and wiggles her toes, almost touching the back of his calves as he continues to stare out the window. Fast-drying. "What are you watching out there?"

"There's a kid in the alley practicing judo or something. He's cute. He has one of those blond bobs like the Hanson brothers."

"How old is he?"

"Dunno. Twelve maybe."

Eliza lies on her back and looks at the ceiling. She painted it blue with clouds one day when Craig wasn't home. Craig hates it, complains about it every time he gets into bed. Sometimes she says, "You don't like it because it wasn't your idea."

"What did you do with your time when you were twelve?" she asks Jude.

"Played Atari games. Ate Fudgee-Os. You?"

"Read *Anne of Green Gables* and thought about being a missionary. I wish someone had taught me judo."

He turns around, belly-flops onto the bed beside her. "I wish someone had taught me to read."

"Don't be coy. I bet you were reading when you were two."

"I couldn't read until I was in the third grade." He presses the side of his face into her pillow, smiles at her with sleepy dark eyes, so close she can smell toothpaste. She wonders if he borrowed her toothbrush, and starts blushing at the thought. Then she wonders how he knew which one was hers. "My parents didn't own any books. They bought me paint-by-number sets and a dog to keep me entertained."

"That doesn't sound so bad. The dog, anyway."

"I hated dogs. I still hate dogs." He turns on his back and kicks his legs toward the ceiling, one after the other. Then he does it again. His boots are already laced on his feet. "It chewed all my shoes and puked on my bed. If I didn't walk it every night they said they'd have it put down. I hated walking at night. There were all these blond Nazi children in the neighbourhood – they looked a lot like that one out there, actually – who used to beat me up."

"Didn't the dog protect you?"

"No. It pissed on my leg and ran."

"Do you hate your parents?"

He stops kicking and lies still. Then he shakes his head. "No, they're all right. They're just perpetually surprised, even after I tell them something seven times. 'You don't like dogs? Why didn't you say so before?'"

The space between them is so small. She turns on her side, props herself on an elbow, and looks at him, the whole length of him down to his boots. "I'm making some tea."

"Not for me, Liza. There's a hole in the bucket."

"How original."

"Craig breaks things."

"I'm going to tell him you were here."

"I know. I don't want to hear what he says."

He pulls himself to his feet, looks out the window again. The back of his head is flattened and awry. Craig's pillow did that to him, she thinks, and almost laughs. Beyond him, beyond the window, the day is too bright to be morning.

When he's gone, she walks around touching things. They didn't touch all night long, just lay there curled up facing one another, talking vaguely until she finished a sentence and he didn't answer. Now she puts fingers on the leaf of the philodendron; the scarred post under the kitchen table, the one the cat uses for scratch practice; the foggy glass of the balcony door. She can see in the texture of the air outside that it's cold.

She sits down at her desk, turns on the computer, opens her thesis file. The last sentence is something she wrote weeks ago, months ago maybe. She doesn't even remember the last time she sat here and did anything but watch the screensaver make strings that she tried to link together into words he might say.

The last thing he said, before he fell asleep, was:

"If I have to choose . . .

. . . I'd rather be your friend."

Craig comes home at two. The coffee is still warm, and he pours himself some. She expected him to be cheerful, to tell her a story about something Tim said over the sound board during the night, to hum her a new melody. Instead he just falls into a chair as though it were a bucket to catch drips.

"What's wrong?" she asks.

"Tim's fucking everything up."

"Like what?"

"He does a mix once, I tell him it's all wrong, he goes into this sulk like I'm his mom telling him to clean his room. He does it again, it's *exactly* the same as the first time, and I try to be patient, and the whole week's wasted. The man thinks he's Mozart on wires. We got nothing done, I'm a wreck, I've got to find myself a new studio but I can't afford anyone else. This is not going to work out."

Eliza sips. The coffee's weak; that isn't going to make him happy either.

"How was your night?" he asks, peering into his coffee as if he's not sure what it is.

"All right. Jude stayed over."

His eyes stay in his coffee cup. She's glad, because she can't help smiling. He smiles too, a little, a knee tapped with a hammer. She hates that smile, his only reaction when he can't think of the correct procedure.

"Oh yeah?"

"Yes."

"I see."

"No you don't. We talked a lot, and then we went to sleep."

He nods, lifting his coffee cup to his mouth, lowering it to his knee. She wonders if it burns him through the frayed threads, then remembers that his coffee and hers are almost the same, and hers is barely warmer than her hands. "What did you talk about? Why was he here, exactly?"

The cat slides under her leg, mews, nudges her with his nose.

"After the party I told him he could stay here. There wasn't any room at Jenny's."

"Did you tell him I wasn't home?"

"Yes."

"And he thought it was another kind of invitation."

"No. He asked if I was sure it'd be okay, and I said I'd like him to come because I'm sometimes scared when I'm here at night and you're not. And we had some tea and talked about school, his thesis and my thesis and all that. And I told him that he could have the couch but that it was uncomfortable, and he could sleep with me if he wanted. And he sort of grinned and said, 'What are you asking me exactly?' And I asked him, 'What do you want me to ask you?' And we were all flirty for awhile, which was kind of awkward, and all that led to us saying we didn't want to do anything that would shut off possibilities."

"I'm feeling right now," says Craig, standing and dropping his coffee cup in the sink with a clang, "that I'd like to shut off a few possibilities."

"You can't be mad."

"Can't I?"

"You've always said you wouldn't care."

"This isn't the same."

"The same as what? As Annette?"

Craig screws his eyes closed and presses his head between his hands. "Every time you hear his voice on the phone you look like someone just granted you three wishes. This is *not* the same."

"So I get my satisfaction in a different way than you do."

He opens his eyes and sighs dramatically. "Annette wasn't about satisfaction. It was curiosity, and I was drunk."

"That's bullshit. You liked her."

Craig stares at her for a long moment. She tries to stare

back, but she can't. She takes a sip of coffee, leans back in her chair, looks at the smudges on the wall that might be newspaper-stained fingerprints, might be crushed from the ends of cigarettes, might be anything.

"You're in *love* with Jude." Craig steps out of the kitchen.

Eliza watches the slicks on the top of her coffee. "That depends on what you mean," she says.

The cat, at the balcony door, doesn't understand that silence is needed.

⫷

A knock. "Liza?"

"I'm in the tub."

"Can I come in?"

She runs a hand on the surface of the water, palm under, top out. "Ummm . . . let me think about that for a minute."

"I'm kidding." Jude's voice is always so light, like oil. "I brought lobster claws. Do you want tea?"

"Lobster claws?"

"You know, the big Italian pastry things with ricotta in them."

"No, I don't know. Are they good?"

"They're a lot like paradise, but messier."

"Perfect. Yes, tea please. On the shelf next to the balcony door."

Her toes are still Toads, chipped now, nostalgic. She got in the bathtub, even though she knew he was coming, because she was cold. She unlocked the front door because she planned to stay there until he arrived, because she thought it would be interesting for him to imagine her in there. She hopes his imagination isn't too much prettier than she is.

"Where's Craig?" Jude calls.

Eliza flips onto her belly and stares into the grit and

puddles on the shelf behind the end of the tub. "Gone to work on the album." It's a grotto in here, the tub sunken into the brick wall and the steps of flaked slate leading up to it. She used to love this bathroom; it was one of the reasons they took the apartment. She's starting to be suspicious of it, though, suspicious of the whole place. Apparently the last people to live here were heroin dealers. She feels something clinging to the decor, something vague, demotivating, artificially soothing. And it costs a fortune to heat, and the upstairs neighbours have a band.

"Can I put on some music?"

"Help yourself. In my office."

Things are always clearest to Eliza when love is leaving. She's noticed this in the past. Love makes her muddled and unreliable; lack of love makes her blind and too eager to please. It's that whiff when she opens the door to let love go that brings her to her senses. This time, though, she wasn't paying attention. As love was going, something else slipped in and set up camp on the couch.

"Boogie Woogie Bugle Boy" creeps under the door. Eliza laughs.

"I wrote today." Jude is standing outside, talking through the door. "I swear, Liza, I'm going to finish this thesis before the spring. You finish too, and then we can run off into the halls of academe together."

"Don't tease." She opens a bottle of almond oil and watches it pour in a thin sunny stream onto the surface of the water. She lifts a puddle of it in her hand; the water runs off her palm and leaves the oil behind in a viscous smear. "My thesis will never be finished. And if it is it will be shit, and no one will ever hire me, and I'll end up being a doctoral bag lady with my cat under my arm. You'll never invite me to your fancy professorial parties full of people who publish in the *PMLA*." She stirs the oil into the bathwater with her hand, which comes up greasy and irritable; the surface of her breasts catches glistening droplets without knowing what to do with them.

"I will. You'll be my token bag lady friend."

The kettle whistle begins its long low moan. She hears him moving around out there, wonders how the floor feels when his soles hit it through his socks, and then there's an odd bang, a bang and a clang heavy and muffled with water, and she wonders, floating, for a long splashing time or so it seems, what such a sound could possibly lead to. It leads to something she never considered. Jude screams.

～

The hospital lasts until night, then through the night, and until night again. She sits in the pistachio waiting room with the grey chairs and drinks coffee that tastes like ashtrays. The phone on the wall is right next to her head, and once, as she nods off, she knocks the receiver and it falls. She picks it up and holds it for a moment. Then she lodges it back where it's supposed to be.

She goes in and Jude is separated from her by pounds of bandages. He opens his eyes and closes them again.

"You should go home," he says.

"Don't be silly."

"You can't help me here, Liza."

There are no windows in this room. Maybe that's why he won't open his eyes.

～

When she gets home, Craig is at the kitchen table. He stares straight at the grey-smudged wall as she drops her bag to the floor.

"You could have called," he says.

"We were at the hospital." She kicks off her shoes, then thinks better of it and jams them back onto her feet.

# A Kettle

"For two days?" He looks at her now. "There's no phone at the hospital? I have been worried. Sick. About. You. Are you all right?"

"Overnight. It's not me. Jude spilled a kettle of boiling water on himself."

"Jesus. Is he okay?"

"No. Yes. He will be." She steps into her office, looks around. There must be something she needs. She grabs a pile of books from the desk and turns back into the kitchen. "He's in a lot of pain and he can't move."

"Is he alone?"

"For the moment. I just came to get some things."

She begins stuffing books into her bag. Craig closes his hand around the pot of the philodendron on the table, tips it to his face as if searching for something among the leaves. "Are you going to move in and be his nursemaid?"

"No. His cousin's coming from Ottawa on Saturday."

"Surely Jude has other friends." She doesn't answer. Craig slams the flowerpot down; Eliza hears a crack. His voice is loud and yet strained, as if it could be much louder if he didn't watch himself. "He can't expect you to look after him for four more days. Why didn't you *call*, for Christ's sake?"

"He doesn't expect anything." She straightens up, folds her arms, tries to take a deep breath. "Craig, don't be this way."

"Doesn't he think you have anything else to do?"

"I *don't* have anything else to do."

"You're supposed to be writing a thesis. You're supposed to have a life. Here."

Eliza bends down and continues pushing books into her bag. Craig, with a gasp of exasperation, bangs his head between his hands on the table. "You don't call, you don't come home, you don't answer my fucking questions." He pulls his head back up, clutching his hair, and watches her, but she refuses to look up, feels his eyes on her like gimlets.

"Is this over, then?" he asks. "Are you going to go be his girlfriend?"

She looks up. Craig turns his head away, toward the window. She follows his eyes and sees that blond kid out in the alleyway. She watches the boy settle his weight solidly on his legs, then dash one foot into the air in front of him. Jude was right; he is cute, wiry, and long-limbed, with that shiny sheaf of hair.

"He doesn't want me to be his girlfriend," she says softly.

Craig nods slowly at the glass. "That is a great comfort to me," he says. "It really is, Eliza."

ॐ

"Liza," Jude says, plucking at a soft white bandage obstinate on his hand, "you don't have to do this."

She says, opening the bottle of Toad, "No, I think I do."

ॐ

What will I do, she sometimes muses, when I'm old, when I get sick, when I need someone to look after me?

But she's not only building karma.

(She read a quote, a few weeks ago, about a button that was around in the sixties: My Karma Ran Over My Dogma. She laughed until she fell off the couch, knocking a lamp onto the hardwood. She read it to Craig, but he'd heard it before and just smiled.)

She doesn't call Craig. She's worried that if she does, no one will answer the phone. Or that he'll answer but neither of them will speak. She can't think of anything she wants to know about him at the moment.

Jude sleeps a lot. She reads books from his shelf, e. e. cummings and Bukowski. The books she brought, for her work, her life, stay in her bag. She makes tea, carefully, but even when he's awake he doesn't want any. She pours it for him, he nods, he says thank you, but then it gets cold on the table beside the bed. She sits next to him, when he's awake, but any words he can manage sound thick and burned.

Occasionally she goes out to get milk or vegetables, never for long. She can feel the days dripping away, and she'll regret it if she wastes them. She has him all to herself now.

One afternoon she lies down next to him while he sleeps. Lies there for a while with Kathy Acker open on her chest, looking up at the ceiling that somebody painted peach-orange. She looks over at him once, his face turned toward her, his lips dry and tentatively closed. Does he even know I'm here? she wonders. It's four o'clock, and already almost dark, through the curtains.

One night she changes the bandages on his hands, his thighs, the skin puckered and peeling like green bark pulling away from red wood. He leaves his underwear on and closes his eyes tight as she dabs oily blue ointment. Under the boiled skin his muscles stay as far away from her fingers as they can.

On Friday he gets out of bed and sits at the kitchen table, grey bandages peeking out of the waistband of his businessman-blue pyjamas, the kind her father used to wear, permanent press in watery colours, dark piping around the pockets. Jude accepts tea, and looks out his own window.

This kitchen, she thinks, is just like mine, the balcony door in the same place, the stove too close to the refrigerator. She imagines a blond prepubescent kicking the air outside the window Jude refuses to look away from.

"I'm leaving tomorrow," she says.

He nods, gives a little sigh into the steam of his cup. His eyes turn toward her. For the first time she sees clearly that there is nothing in them but himself.

"You did say we'd be friends," she says, and her stomach fills with sickness.

"We are," he replies.

The sky outside the window is a thick, opaque blue like a turquoise stone, and too close, like it's dropped toward the ground during the night. She can see red leaves against it, somewhere in the distance. A plane chugs past, flashing a little.

"It was my kettle," she says, placing her hands flat on the table, not daring to be too close. "It was my kitchen."

૨/

On Saturday morning she puts her things back into her bag and then makes breakfast: scrambled eggs with spinach, toast, and jam. Jude smiles, eats. They look at each other for long moments, open their mouths decorated with crumbs.

"I'll call you in a couple of days," Jude says as she gets up to go. He glances at her quickly, then looks away. "I'm feeling better and better all the time."

She thinks, with a pulse of horror, that she might cry. I was going to take care of him, she thinks. Even when he just slept next to me in my bed, I was never going to ask for anything that he didn't want to give me. I was going to wait for him.

She leaves by the balcony door, leaving it open, skittering down the fire-escape steps like a bug, surprised by her own grace. At the bottom she stops and looks up at the window. She imagines him looking out at her and humming. *There's a hole in the bucket.*

૨/

When she gets home there's no one there, no note, no sign. The air is vacant and still, as though nothing in there but the cat, close to the floor, has moved for days.

She takes off her coat, puts down her bag, and walks the length of the apartment and back again. She looks at everything as deeply as she can – the rice-paper shades on the lamps, the pile of books next to the bed, the litterbox in the closet, the silent computer on the desk. She doesn't touch. She takes off her clothes, pulls on her bathrobe, turns the water on to fill the tub. She sits down at the desk, turns on the computer, looks at the strings of the screensaver. Then she becomes aware of the cat shrieking, and goes to fill its empty bowl. She watches it gobble, and then lets it out onto the balcony. She leans against the doorframe and watches the morning turning into afternoon.

Below her, in the alleyway, the boy is punching invisible enemies. He stops moving, breathing hard, his hands on bent knees, blond hair all over his face.

She stands still in the doorway for a moment, and then darts onto the balcony. She tumbles down the fire escape in her bare feet and bathrobe, almost kicking the cat over the stairs; it mutters and shoots back up to the safety of the landing. At the bottom she trips and falls into the boy's eyeline, landing on one knee. He straightens, speechless, watching her with large aquamarine eyes. She picks herself up and brushes her knees; beads of blood push through her skin.

"My name's Eliza," she says.

The boy moves his weight onto one leg slightly, as though to spring away. She lifts her fingertips in panic – don't go.

"I live up there." She gestures. "I have breakfast by the window. I sometimes see you in the morning. Is that judo, what you're doing?"

His eyes flicker around; his lips shift. "Kung fu," he replies. His voice is like a woman's, but rustier.

"You must be very serious about it."

"Yeah."

"What's your name?"

He doesn't answer.

Love is leaving, she thinks. The door is opening, but nothing is approaching from the other side.

"Would you teach me something?" she asks. "Something easy."

He looks to one side and then the other, his yellow bob flopping. "I think I have to go."

"Just something small. Teach me how to stand."

"Sorry."

He turns his back and crosses the nearest lawn, goes in the back door. Eliza watches the door a long time. Nothing comes out, and she can't go in. But she feels, with unusual acuity, her body pressing through the soles of her bare feet into the earth. So she stands a little longer, looks down at the Toads of her toenails, then along the alley to the place where it meets the road.

When she starts to shiver, she turns and goes back up the fire escape stairs. The cat is waiting for her at the top, pawing at the crack of the balcony door, which of course has shut and locked behind her.

# Just Ahead
# of Us
# in Line

That summer I was so thin that everything fit perfectly. I was twenty-two years old and I ran away to Montreal and got a job as a cashier at Le Chateau. José with the little round glasses, such a sweet-looking boy, said he'd like to take me down to the lunch room and slam me against the wall. We took all our breaks together and his girlfriend started freaking out. I was dying to go to bed with him, but he found it more exciting to talk about it.

Skinny Patrizia and I stood around in the endless warehouse folding sweaters and hanging up velour dresses and talking about my roommate Enrico, with whom I was in love, and Nico, the second cousin Trizie hadn't seen for two years, since he'd moved back to Italy with his family.

When I think about throwing up my food, I'm usually thinking of that summer. It seemed I was so beautiful that nothing I could do was wrong.

I'm listening to Carrie's breathing and trying to make my breath follow hers. For the first time in many years, I remember lying on the sofa curled in close to my mother and feeling her breasts and throat moving in and out with her air, and me trying to match my air to hers. I never could; I still can't, lying here wrapping Carrie the way a cherry leaf wraps a rice cake. I never understand how people can breathe so quickly.

When I fall asleep, I dream about Patrizia.

I see her accidentally, in a dark street outside one of those loud neon dance bars we used to go to. I know it's her because I feel something rise up in me, that particular sensation that is always her, although this feeling is more than she's ever been before. Her faint moustache has vanished, and her face is now fine and impatient. Her limbs seem browner and longer and careless, not knobby as they were, but smooth and strong. She's wrapped in a forgettable dress. Maybe her feet are bare.

I breathe "Trizie" in the way I've imagined breathing other names if their owners reappeared unexpectedly. She sees me, and her blankness takes a little turn. She looks as if she's been waiting for me, not entirely gladly. Her hazel eyes are bright and heavy.

"You haven't been around," she says, letting her sheet of black hair fall over her face and around her breasts.

I clasp her upper arm with one hand. "Trizie." I don't pretend I'm not pleading. "Come home with me."

I said this to her once in real life, but it didn't mean what it means now. She shakes her head. "If you follow me," she says, "I won't stop you from coming in. But I'm not inviting you."

I follow her.

Her upstairs apartment is crowded with battered objects: statuettes of owls, half-dead plants, armchairs. In the living room, José is sitting on a slumping couch, setting up a game of MasterMind on the low coffee table. Patrizia vanishes into what I suppose is the kitchen.

"Where'd she go?" I ask.

"She's hiding," he says. "She does that a lot. Play?"

I sit down. "I wanted to call her. I thought about calling her."

"You can call me any time you want, baby." Patrizia is sitting next to me, drooping, her eyes excited but the rest of her too sad to care. "But no time soon. I don't want to be all mixed up with you again any time soon."

I look at her not looking at me. "It's amazing, Trizie. I was the one you said only a man made of stone could resist. And now here I am all fat and scared, and all the desperation is for you. How did this happen?"

I look at José, who's watching her. I think maybe he watched her differently, before I arrived.

When I wake up, I get up, careful not to disturb the woman of my life, the one who saved me from bad men like Enrico. I dial the phone before I lose my nerve. When a woman answers the phone "*Oui?*" I ask for Patrizia. She doesn't answer for a moment. Then she says, in an affronted voice, that Patrizia now lives in Notre-Dame-de-Grâce with her husband. She won't give me the number, and doesn't ask who I am. I remember Nico's name, though, and he's in the telephone book.

I'm feeling a lot like I did that summer on the beach, in high school, in that place where Carrie and I grew up. I was in love with Sean that summer, and he was in love with Dinah. Some boys from the next camp canoed down and our boys wanted to borrow their boats. The others said: "What'll you give us?" Our boys said: "Whaddya want?" The others turned to look up the beach, and there was Dinah in her blue bathing suit (nicely modest so everyone would know that she was less of a slut than I was and didn't have to try as hard). The boys said: "*Her.* We want her." Carrie, who was just as pretty as Dinah and turned out to be far prettier, said: "Smile, Dinah, give them a little wave." Dinah giggled and she smiled and she waved.

Carrie became my friend much later, even though when she was a kid we all said she was a brat, and when she grew up we all turned green because of the way her body went straight up and down. A couple of years ago, when Carrie and I were in London for completely different reasons, I called her up because she was a girl from home, and we went to a play, and then we went dancing with some of her friends and she threw her long hair around, and I thought: you are so cool and you are so beautiful. By then I had forgotten all about Dinah. I suspect Carrie never did. We never forget the one who's just ahead of us in line at any given time.

Patrizia's legs, I see when she twists and her skirt pulls up, are heavier than mine. At least, that's what I think. I'm never sure exactly how big any part of me is. Her face, which used to be pointed, has developed soft curves, roundish cheeks, an extra chin when she pulls the original one back. I can see the beginnings of her upper arms, loose under her short sleeves. Her hair is longer than before, past her backside, and there are little wires of grey. I'm looking at her legs and she sees me doing it, but I can't stop. It's all there, everything I've ever hated about myself: the ripples pressing through muscle fibre, the snaky white stretch marks, the jiggle when she shifts, the bulges against the hem of her short skirt. I'm so relieved. The hard core of my desperation is softening, wilting, decomposing. She didn't even bother to flatter herself, to cover up what shouldn't show. Her belly is pushing, her bare arms are dimpled, she isn't wearing a brassiere. I start to congratulate myself.

She's watching, her eyes green-amber tea. I scan her face, looking for familiar things: the thin-lipped wide mouth, the nose turned up at the tip, the trace of a black moustache. The dream I had about her was far more like her than this woman is.

We both smile. I think of asking her what happened to José, but there's no reason she would know.

Walking home, I have a vision of my mother. I often do, and she usually says: If you weighed a hundred and ten pounds you'd be as beautiful as any of the most beautiful women you know.

When I get home, Carrie's making dinner, and I sit down to watch her.

When I met up with Carrie in London, I was trying to decide whether or not to run away from Enrico. Carrie was there because she was going to be a dancer, and she'd met a man who was going to teach her how. She started dancing because not eating wasn't enough; she had to get rid of what was already there, and what managed to sneak its way in to keep her from dying.

Carrie and I have always shared a difficulty with food. That is, we always shared the fact of difficulty; our difficulties were different. Carrie was a normal child who liked potato chips and Oreos until she was fourteen or so, when she stopped eating for a number of years. Several times her parents made her sit all night at the dinner table, and tried to make her swallow the cold kidneys and string beans in the morning. Finally, she stopped going to dinner.

I always wanted to be like that. I tried, I'm still trying, to live on dry toast and spoonfuls of yoghurt and the occasional raw vegetable and cup after cup of black coffee, but I couldn't, I can't, if I don't get myself those *oeufs florentins* for breakfast I'll be thinking about them all day and into the night, and although I'll hate myself once they're in me, at least I'll be able to get something done.

When we talked about moving in together, in London, she made a declaration to me: she would not cook. She had never learned to cook, and she wouldn't learn, ever. She said: "You'll do the cooking. I'll wash the dishes. I will not, *not* become one of those women who can baste the perfect pot roast, who can measure a quarter-teaspoon of salt in the palm of her hand. I won't be that. Not ever."

Her mother was one of those women. Straight out of a kitchenware ad. Her home was always as clean and pretty as the hothouse daisies sprayed with water in the florist's shop at the mall. There was always an odour of something tasty (often pot roast, as a matter of fact, but sometimes cookies or mushroom soup or Red Rose tea), but it never overcame the whiff of Windex or floor wax or vinegar.

I didn't mind being designated cook. I liked cooking. I believed that when Carrie smelled my hand-kneaded bread and took a look at my spinach lasagne, she would stop being afraid, and would smile at me adoringly as she licked her plate clean.

And yet, in the end, she got better without my help, and I have never cooked anything for her. I poured her granola she didn't eat, on the mornings she and I sat in my kitchen in London, both trying to be indifferent. In the two years we've been together I've never made her anything, not even a birthday card. She has, for me: she painted me a picture when I finally decided to leave Enrico; she knitted me a scarf one Christmas. But making her dinner, making her presents, would have seemed like an admittance. I always had plans to cook for her some day, when all the blueprints we'd drawn for our life together became solid objects. But it hasn't really happened. She has learned to like food again, and I had no hand in it. And she learned to cook, so she doesn't need me.

Now I sit on a chair in our kitchen and watch her wielding a cleaver – clumsily, but she never misses – over a carrot, while beside her the pan grows fat with vegetables. She's splashing oil and rosemary about as though it's no more complicated than walking upstairs. She isn't talking to me, but she isn't concentrating, either; I can't catch her eyes ever resting on what her hands are doing. When everything is tossed and sprinkled and the pan is in the oven, she starts constructing a *spanakopita*, slowly but rhythmically. I watch, trying not to look fascinated, then deciding it's okay if I am. I don't think she wants any questions, though. I don't think she wants to be reminded of the things we used to say to each other.

The oven and that big cleaver frighten me now.

I can't sleep. In the living room, on my way to a glass of water, I notice a big, heavy photo album with a hand-woven cover, tucked into the newspaper catcher under the three-bulbed lamp. It's never been there before. I get my water, and then I sit down on the sofa and pull the book to me. The pages are black paper.

All the photos are black and white, and all are of Carrie. Some have other people in them, too – one man in particular is there often, a man not quite as tall as her, strong-looking and lean, able to lift her over his head on the flats of his two hands. We were never properly introduced, but I know who he is; I remember seeing him once or twice, at those big faceless parties Carrie sometimes had in London. In the picture of him lifting her, Carrie's completely swathed, face and all – mummified – in a cloth that looks, in the black-and-white photo, coldly grey. I know it's her from the length and breadth of her, and because she has to be in the picture somewhere.

In another photo, we see her from one side, naked and bound. The soles of her feet are flat on the crown of her head.

Her ankles are joined to her neck by a taut loop of rope under her chin. Her arms are behind her, between her legs and parallel to her knees, wrists tied together. Her body forms a jagged, bumpy wheel, almost a teardrop; her breasts are strained little conehills with nipples so hard they hurt me. Her hair is dyed shocking black. There is a white, frayed gag in her mouth.

Then there's another picture, small and vague. I take it out of its black paper corners and squint at it. It's just her face, her bony face, with huge opaque eyes that look up at me almost smiling, and her wrists, proffered, black with blood.

〜

I only met Patrizia's family once. She'd explained to me that they hit her sometimes, but that it wasn't really their fault; when her older brother died they kind of went to pieces, and she didn't help by talking back and getting angry all the time. I asked her why she didn't have her own place. She said maybe she would someday, but it would really make everyone crazy. No nice Italian girl she knew would think of running off on her own when she had two loving parents to look after her.

Her father sat me down at the kitchen table and asked me questions like: "How do you manage then, a working girl living with a man, with all the cooking and cleaning to do?" and then: "What kind of girl are you?" after which her mother shouted at her in Italian, and I could understand that she was saying: "The Bible says honour thy father and thy mother," and I understood Trizie to reply: "And the daughter? What about the daughter?" and I waited for her as she went upstairs to gather all the money she had – five hundred and fifty dollars – and I heard her mother shout at her in French: "You can't go work at that store any more, you're meeting all sorts of bad people, you'll stay right here and we'll give you what you need, it's no kind of life for a girl like you."

Patrizia stormed out of the house and I followed her, almost ashamed because of the things they were saying about me. She cried a little and I held onto her. I said, "Trizie, come home with me. You can stay with Enrico and me for as long as you want." And she sobbed, "Maybe I will. Maybe I will."

But soon she wiped her face and pulled her spine up straight, and her jade-brown eyes looked away toward the house that held her parents inside. She said, "They're taking me to Italy this summer. If I don't go with them, I might never see Nico again."

After we went dancing, she went home. I went home too, and called my mother, even though it was late. I told her about Trizie, and she said, "Sounds like she was taught all the wrong priorities." I suddenly had to cry with a rage so helpless that I hung up the phone without saying goodbye.

I call Patrizia and ask her to come to dinner. She pauses and then says . . . I'm just noticing this now, the difference between her voice long ago and her voice now. Those days when we danced with the broom behind the jewelry counter to "La Isla Bonita," her voice was raucous. It reminded me of the laughter of those girls who stood outside the warehouse in red satin and fishnets with holes. Whenever we left work after nine they'd be there, some of them beautiful, although some had big wobbly asses or acne. We'd hear them laughing in tones very different from those they used with the men who pulled along slowly without really stopping. When they talked to each other, their laughing was almost girlish, edging close to who they were when they leaned against their lockers at recess and talked about who could buy them beer next weekend.

Those girls outside the warehouse could have turned out to be us.

Now, when she says, "Nico's going to be out of town this weekend, so maybe I can come then. . . ." that note in her voice – that note of remembering, of belief that she exists – is gone.

I consider asking Carrie to make dinner, because I don't think I can, and because I want to be sure she won't carefully forget that she's promised to be there. But she says, "Patrizia. Yeah. Sure, I'd like to meet her." Then she busies herself with something and it seems like unforgivable presumption to ask her to cook.

On Saturday morning, I settle into the big soft armchair in the kitchen with a bowl of café au lait and a plate of toast and cheese and take out Carrie's favourite cookbook. I find something that doesn't look too scary: tomato sauce with olives. I remember making that often a long time ago, when I lived with Enrico and he said he liked it. I go to the organic grocery store on the corner, and for once I skip the fridge full of hummus and pesto in plastic tubs. I go instead to the piles of vegetables, orange and green, long or round, not as shiny as they used to be in the supermarket where I bought things for Enrico. I fill my basket nervously, stopping on the way to the cash to grab some Parmigiano-Reggiano, the one Enrico always insisted on.

I'm remembering now, the moment I stopped making food. It was the morning after Patrizia grabbed her five hundred and fifty dollars and almost came home with me; the morning after I decided not to talk to my mother any more ever again. It was the morning I woke up and told Enrico that something was wrong and I wasn't sure we'd be able to fix it. I didn't leave him that morning, or even for months after. But I got up the next day with the intention of making Sunday morning waffles and threw up in the toilet instead.

I decided to go to London because it was far away. I never cooked anything again, and when I came back to Montreal I brought Carrie with me, and I never went back to work at Le Chateau.

꙰

The three of sit at the kitchen table in silence, twirling our undercooked noodles, and I ask Carrie, "Do you have any idea what ever happened to Dinah?"

Patrizia doesn't look up. She's chewing deeply, caring only about the flavour of olives and musty cheese. I'm not sure Carrie's heard me, but then she swallows and says, "Who?"

"Dinah," I repeat. "Don't you remember Dinah from summer camp?"

Carrie leaves her fork near her closed mouth and looks at the greyish wall opposite her, behind Patrizia's mound of form, for a while, as if hoping some face called Dinah will emerge from it. "Dinah from summer camp. Summer camp in high school?"

"Yes. Don't you remember that day on the beach, when the boys came down in their canoes. . .?"

Carrie's eyes, not her face, turn toward me. She's tired. She has hollows in all sorts of unnatural places. She puts the forkful of noodles in her mouth. "This is delicious. I wish you'd cook more. Dinah. . . ."

I want to cry: The one they all wanted first, and you second.

I look at Patrizia, who's not listening. I wonder, with a series of twinges which follow each other like small, identical boats skimming slowly from around a corner of a beach, if, when Patrizia heard my voice on the phone after so many years, my face emerged vaguely from the wall before her, half-remembered.

As I look at her not looking at either of us, I wonder if I'm still half-remembered, if she only half-remembers herself, skinny and laughing like a high school girl, dancing behind the jewelry counter to "La Isla Bonita." Or if she remembers, at all, the things we used to say to one another. Things like: *Come home with me.*

# It Tastes Sweet

These rocks are full of faces. The Japanese word for "goblin" is *tengu*. It starts with the rock at the waterfall, the rock that looks like an elephant. Around the rock is a pool the colour of hematite. Matthew says, "In summer we jumped from up here. It's deep enough." The waterline is four metres below us. I wonder how cold it is. The surface is absolutely still and reflective.

Matthew says, "The water in the pool in the Yucatan was sweet. It tasted sweet."

He's told me about the pool in the Yucatan before, but very few of Matthew's stories stay with me. The things about Matthew that stay with me are: his willingness to let me walk with an arm around his waist; the long solidness of his limbs; the helplessness of his orgasms all quivering and surprised.

I'm meeting Gregory in Kansai airport one week from today. I remember only pieces of him, mostly his eyes, which he says were once cold and hard. They weren't when I saw them, although the rest of him was.

It's less than a jump; a jump would be a decision. I remember Freud's adage that vertigo is the struggle against the desire to hurl oneself into the abyss. I've always loved vertigo.

For a second or two I'm submerged, my eyes closed. It's not silent inside; it's the fullest my ears can be, liquid sound, sound as substance. Then I come out into the air, which is much worse.

I'm wearing two wool sweaters and jeans. My hair is vining my face. All around me are rocks, pale grey and cold and dusty like elephants, curious and not helpful. The only place that will let me out is much too far away. I go under again. This is not the ocean; there's no movement, only cold. Only a green colour, like "go." This is not the places I went to as a child, where there was water. This is far colder, and complacent.

The place where I come up is nearer the place that will let me out. Matthew is standing above me, on the grey that is like ice. That thing his body does during orgasm – his eyes are doing it now. If you come down here we'll both die, I think. The water is indeed very deep, and meanly calm. I take a breath and sink, my lazy sweaters dragging me down. My hand, suddenly panicked, touches stone in front of me.

I won't let Matthew help, afraid that whatever got me will get him too. There's a welcoming space for my fingers, and another for the toes of my sneakers. The water is indifferent, but the air's angry enough to kill me. I stand while Matthew pulls off my sweaters, my running shoes, my socks, my jeans, my thermals the colour of the rocks. Then he strips off his jacket and wraps it around me. Normally he might be strong enough to carry me back to the car, but something's gone from him, so he merely holds me up as I walk.

"I slipped," I say.

I get into the back seat and cry silently as he drives back to the villa.

Next it's the faces in the caves. There are lights that the caves didn't invite. The men behind me are delighted when I read a few of the simplest *kanji* aloud.

The word for "water" in Japanese is *mizu*, or sometimes *sui*. The picture that means "water" looks like water, like an artfully arranged fountain that appears to be random but is always the same. There is water in these caves. I can hear it, speaking to me in little plunks and dark drips. I touch my nose to a low-hanging stalactite and viscous, warm liquid slips to my cheek and down along my chin.

The pools here aren't meant to be; I can see black eel-like pipes trying to be inconspicuous. I like them anyhow, these pools, still yet shivering like the surface of a bubble.

I imagine being very small, the size of a rosy carp or even smaller, being able to swim amongst these goblin faces and stone icicles in all their mosses and golds and leopard-pelt mottles, finding what's in those dark passages just high enough to reach above the water's skin.

Matthew's leaving me behind. This is understandable. I have not earned the effort it would take for him to have any notion of what's wrong with me. Sometimes I catch glimpses of him through the passages. He's holding himself very straight today, and trying to look concerned without looking into my face.

The time I visited Gregory in his Osaka apartment, he gave me a packet of Indonesian clove cigarettes and we stood on his balcony while I smoked, and as we looked far down upon his neighbours going in and out on their bicycles and on their feet, I told him what Freud said about vertigo. Gregory said, "That's it. That's exactly it."

Matthew knows about Gregory, but Matthew doesn't know a thing about vertigo.

I put a hand on the wet greasy wall and it comes away smelling of mold. This is okay, the smell of things growing in

81

the dark. There aren't really supposed to be lights. Matthew has probably gone out the other side. I let the delighted men pass by and stand looking into the maze of goblins. I wish I could stay here and learn about these faces, learn what it's like to never move, never see the sun, what it's like to just slowly wear away.

The water from the mineral spring tastes sweet. Matthew points this out and I nod and smile. "It tastes sweet," he says again. I remember the story now, about a man he met somewhere on the Yucatan who took him swimming in a pool where the water tasted sweet, and then the man asked Matthew to come spend the night with him and Matthew was so imbued with the sweetness of the water that he almost said yes. But he didn't.

I'm not sure why Matthew told me this story.

The things about Gregory that stay with me are: several three-hour phone conversations, a packet of Indonesian clove cigarettes – I still have the box – and a refrain that I believe: *I can't talk to anyone but you.*

Matthew's filling up the jugs while I watch, and I'm putting my hands against the stones. We don't need this water – there's plenty coming out of the taps in the villa – but there's something different about it here. Something Matthew's been looking for.

# Be Well, Whatever

It's hot. Hannah hears Dwayne's voice under the window, and the voice of her friend Michael, his friend Michael. Their voices are irritable with sweat.

She's kicked off the sheets and she's lying, sticky. She's slept without clothes for years now, and she knows Dwayne sneaks in to look at her at night. Once when she woke up he was touching her, and she sat up like a party hooter unrolling straight and noisy, and he was so scared when she yelled that he buried himself in his lap and wouldn't move, foolish like an ostrich. He was scared; that was what she thought, and felt proud. Only years later will she understand what he was really hiding.

After that there was no more touching that she knew of. She still saw him through her lashes, though, standing in the doorway. Her mother bought her nightgowns, but she wouldn't wear them. She couldn't sleep, but she wouldn't let him make her wear them.

When Hannah started going to school, she learned that life begins in September. August burns itself out in a fury of white sunshine, dares about leaping from the balcony, tanned and frightened kisses. You sink into the pool and hold your breath until the year dies. Then you buy a pack of coil-bound exercise books and some new jeans printed with roses. Baptismal gifts. She feels new in September, and everything around her celebrates the newness with her, except the people who live in her house. Last year her mother made the same thing for supper on the last day of summer and the first day of school. It's all the same fucking day, man; that's how her mother would have put it years ago. Hannah sat and looked at the spaghetti with meat sauce and the saucer piled high with soft, damp, factory-sliced beige-brown bread and decided that if she didn't eat, she'd trick the curse her mother was trying to lay. Dwayne was there across the table, staring and wolfing and saying, "She must be on a diet again." Her mother grew steadily more bitter silent, and finally leaned into Hannah's face and, with a curl of her lip, said softly, "She can make her own fucking supper from now on if that's how she feels." Hannah went upstairs and closed her bedroom door, the door that doesn't keep anybody out.

Hannah doesn't get up; she listens to Michael's voice. "Dwayne, buddy," he says, "there's no way it'll all fit. You never listen to me, man. You have to figure out another way."

Hannah hears the heave and shuffle of things being hoisted in and out of the back of Michael's rickety truck, the one with the leaks in the roof. She and Michael sat there in the rain once and got dripped on while Michael said things about love over and over, said that she was just running away from him. They've almost all been like that: trying to tell her that she only imagines that she doesn't want things. The ones she does want look incredulous, and walk away.

It's only morning now; it'll be late afternoon before he goes. It's never been just Hannah and her mother before. When Dwayne arrived, Daddy was here too. Dwayne was the only addition ever; after that everything started to drip away, oil draining into paper. Leaving her cold, congealing.

The clock says nine. She swings her legs over the side of the bed, but the rest of her can't move. Getting up is always the worst thing that happens to her all day. She remembers being six, seven, eight years old, when school was no longer a novel thing that made her want to be awake, sitting on the end of her bed trying to get dressed. Sometimes a sock would be half on and she'd have to stop, sit there, her head hanging almost to her knees, her fingers slowly releasing elastic. Sometimes her mother came in, and Hannah made some attempt to move, managed to get that sock up over her ankle, while her mother stood in the door and watched. Hannah didn't turn to look, but could feel her mother's arms clenched across her breasts, her lips held together with her teeth. Sometimes her mother grabbed her and stood her roughly on her feet, yanking a dress over her head. Or a turtleneck sweater; Hannah believed her mother chose the turtlenecks on purpose. Hannah was terrified of the way they clamped over her face, thought she'd get stuck there and would never get at the air again. On some days Hannah cried, "Hold it open hold it open!" and her mother laughed and stretched the neck so Hannah's face could slip through easily, not even touching. But on the mornings when Hannah knew she was nothing but a stone dragging her mother to the ocean floor, she couldn't even raise her head. If she spoke, God only knew what might happen.

Hannah pulls herself to her feet. She drags on a plain white T-shirt that doesn't suit her – it's shapeless, the collar is too round – and some shorts that hang down to her knees. They were once cotton pants; now strings droop from the edges, black against her chalky calves, over her sweat. She twists her hair into a tangled topknot in a greasy elastic. Maybe she's sexy this way: dishevelled, careless, confident. She doesn't look in the mirror. Rubbing her face with the palms of her hands, she takes the stairs one at a time.

When she was very small she used to hurry down

staircases, but early on she realized that a staircase is an interim place. She started sitting on stairs, listening to the reality below, whether it was her parents laughing and drinking whiskey with their brothers and sisters or their friends, or Dwayne and the neighbourhood boys loudly telling tales about the girls in their seventh-grade class – who would kiss behind the Anglican church, which one already had big tits. One boy saying, "Dwayne, man, that baby cousin of yours is fucking cute." Dwayne saying, "She still wets the bed, man, her room always smells of semen." "What's semen? You mean dried piss? Isn't she, like, nine or ten or something?" "Yeah, man, it's gross. She's weird, she's always trying to touch me."

Michael is in the kitchen. "Hannah, hi," he says. He grabs a coffee mug from the cupboard and fills it with cold water. Dwayne comes in behind him. They're almost the same height – high – and about the same width – not wide, with knobby bones at their wrists and collars. They both have faintly gingerish hair, and freckles.

"You look like crap," Dwayne says in her direction. "It's embarrassing." Michael drains the water from the cup and fills it again.

"It's none of your business what I look like."

Through the window is the old apple tree in the front yard, the one whose yellowish, withered apples suck all the moisture from your mouth. When she and Dwayne and her mother first moved to this house, after Daddy died, Hannah took her book out to that tree and climbed it. She'd heard and read so much about trees being their own little worlds, places where you could forget that anyone else was alive. But there was nowhere to put her back, and there were caterpillars.

She needs something to do, so she goes to the refrigerator and takes out the orange juice. On the day Dwayne arrived, when she and he sat on either side of the kitchen table glancing excitedly and nervously at one another, Hannah's mother had asked them if they'd like juice and what kind of juice they'd like. They both said, "Orange juice!" in the same breath. Then they grinned at each other. They knew that these details were the most important in any friendship, and that no matter what unbearable things might happen, these particulars – orange juice, a tendency to nearsightedness, a secret – would keep them with one another forever.

"I'm outta here," Dwayne sings, grabbing the orange juice carton from her hand before she finishes pouring. Juice spills on her T-shirt. "Oops, sorry," he yelps, and then giggles. "Sorry, sorry, you're just too slow. Gotta get a move on. It's almost time to go." He's pleased with his little rhyme and repeats it, singsong.

"Sorry
Sorry
Hannah's too slow.
Gotta get a move on
It's time to go."

Michael's watching her, and when she looks at him he gives a small, hesitant smile and looks away. I wonder, she thinks. I wonder if he's been waiting for the breakdown, for three to become two. She feels a bit sick. She's told Michael over and over; at first she tried not to say it, because she knew it was cruel, but finally there was no other way. *I don't love you. Michael, I don't love you.* But he keeps asking her, telling her, instructing her on how he's going to save her from herself. From her life. He doesn't know – and he may be shocked, even pained, to discover it – that as of today, she is saved.

Hannah sits at the kitchen table with her orange juice clenched in one hand, wishing to God they'd go away and stop looking at her, stop making her feel like she takes up space. "She's lost weight," Dwayne says, taking a swig from the carton. "I think she might turn into a normal girl someday."

"Why would she want to be a normal girl?" Michael folds his hands on the table primly, like a middle-aged minister asking kind, jovial questions about slightly embarrassing things. "If more girls were like her, people like you and me would have more friends. She's special, our Hannah."

"Oh, fuck you, Michael." Hannah sighs. "You don't know anything about me."

"No, but I do." Dwayne grins.

She stands, goes to the sink, and dumps her orange juice down the drain. She feels filthy, greasy, as though smeared with menstrual blood and cooking fat, rolled in the dust on the kitchen floor. She heads for the stairs, hearing Michael behind her asking, "Why are you always such a shit to her?" and Dwayne answering, "She's just too fucking sensitive. She thinks she's a goddamn princess."

Hannah goes into her mother's bathroom and takes the bottle of special shower gel. Later her mother will discover the wet soapy bottle and tell Hannah to buy her own bath stuff, selfish brat. Her mother owns certain things; shower gel, potato chips, writing paper, are *hers*. Hannah needs to take these things occasionally, hoping her mother won't notice and hoping she will.

She can see the truck full of Dwayne's things from the bathroom window. She peels off her clothes, already damp with sweat, and climbs into the bathtub, which is stained with grey smudges under her feet. She turns the shower on while she's standing under it, and it smacks her with a blast of cold. She gives a brief brittle scream, and then she cries.

She doesn't cry well; she never has. Her chest feels like it's wrapped in iron bands. The weight of her breasts is dragging the top of her down to the floor. She can imagine how ugly her face is, uglier still with the effort of trying to keep it in, to stop, like her mother's face the night Daddy died. Hannah decided that night that she wouldn't cry because she didn't want her face to look like that.

She pours sweet-sharp flowery gel onto a washcloth and starts to rub it over her skin, afraid she'll hurt herself if she rubs too hard. She considers touching herself between the legs, but then no. Whatever she might release that way needs to stay with her today.

She stands in the shower until she's shivering too hard to cry anymore. Then she stands on the mat, dripping. There's old polish on her fingernails and she peels it off, slowly, letting pale shimmery flakes snow down to the floor. Dwayne and Michael come up the stairs, muttering at one another in tense, clipped tones. Dwayne pounds on the door. "What the hell are you doing? You're not the only person in this house. I'm in a *hurry.*"

"Go away," Hannah says, and she stands there for a little longer.

She considers putting on her ugly, sweaty clothes before going out, but she won't. She won't let them make her. She wraps herself in a towel and her hair in another, and marches out quickly, down the hall to her bedroom. Dwayne and Michael are in his room, shovelling stuff back and forth, their backs to the door. They don't notice her.

She goes into her bedroom and pulls out some things. The striped pastel billowy skirt with the small waist, which her mother bought her last week because she lost five more pounds. Her little pink T-shirt that pulls her breasts in just right. She puts on some lip gloss and brown eye pencil before drying her hair all cloudy with the hair dryer.

And now what? It's not the first time a day has been all about waiting for the end of it, but this is the first time it's been so urgent, so endless. He's leaving at five o'clock. At six o'clock maybe Hannah and her mother will order Kentucky Fried Chicken and rent a video. For the first time in all eternity the two of them will be alone together. Hannah can hear her mother's voice downstairs. She darts out to the bathroom, plucks up the bottle of shower gel, and slips into her mother's bathroom to put it back where it came from. Then she goes down and out to the front step.

"Hannah." Her mother is standing on the path on the front lawn. "Do you think you could help your cousin with his things?" Her hands are on her hips; she raises one of them, and her eyebrows, in her I-don't-know-why-I-always-have-to-state-the-obvious expression.

"There's not much point, Mrs Evans." Michael pushes his ginger bangs out of his face. "The truck's full. Dwayne just has too much. He's going to have to leave some stuff behind."

It's almost noon. The sun is unbearable. Hannah turns around and slips inside, puts her back against the cool glass of the screen door. Outside her mother is saying, "Dwayne, I told you to send some things by mail. Come inside and tape some of those boxes up. I'll mail them when you know your address."

"I need this stuff *now*."

Her mother sighs with a short puff. "You don't, not everything. Come on."

"Stop telling me what to think," Dwayne barks.

Her mother's voice is stiff and dangerous. "Prepare them properly to be sent or I'll throw them away. Or give them to Hannah."

"Do what you want." Dwayne slams the back of the truck. "Just don't give me fucking orders."

Against Hannah's back, the door jerks open; she almost falls out onto the step. Her mother slams past her and up the stairs. Something drops to the ground with a crash.

"That's it, Dwayne, man," Michael shouts, with a clang of hurled keys. "Forget it. You can do your own fucking moving. Unload, go get a van, bring the truck to me when you're done. I'm sick of you and I'm going home." Hannah hears him scuffle out the driveway and down the road, yelling over his shoulder.

"And when you get there, you can make yourself some new fucking friends. Hannah and me, we're done with you, you fucking loser."

Then everything's quiet. Through the window in the door Hannah sees a slight movement of wind in the leaves. It's the first wind all day. Upstairs, her mother is moving around in the bathroom. "God*dammit*, Hannah, you used my fucking bath gel again."

Hannah opens the door.

On the path on the front lawn, on the steps that lead to the driveway, in the shadow of the tree with the inedible apples, is Dwayne. He's sitting with his ginger head in his hands, his elbows on his lap, and he's crying. Hannah can't see his face; she's glad she can't see his face. His back is heaving. She wonders what would happen if she moved closer, but she stays still, and doesn't let the screen door close for fear he'll hear. He drops his head into his lap, wraps his arms around his shins, and sobs, looking about eight years old. But then, no. He looks about fifteen, about her age. He looks like he did that night when she finally woke up, trying to hide parts of himself inside other parts. He straightens up and dries his face with the tail of his shirt, and sits still for a moment, rigid. Then he stands, and climbs into the cab of the truck.

As he pulls the door shut he sees her. For a moment he stares. Then he jabs the key into the ignition and turns it. The motor jerks, and he raises a hand. "So long, Hannah. Be well. Whatever." He spins out the driveway, spraying gravel over the piles of boxes he leaves strewn behind him.

Hannah looks at the driveway for awhile. Then she walks to the end of the path and sits on the step. Her organs are doing all sorts of tricky, unfathomable things, and she's trying to make them be still. The only other time she's seen him cry, since the day he arrived at the age of nine, was the night a year ago when Michael got alcohol poisoning and ran the truck into the side of his own house. Hannah and Dwayne sat in the waiting room with Michael's mother while the doctor explained the mechanics of comas. Hannah stared at the white chalk surfaces of the backs of her hands, but Dwayne kept his head down, and when he finally lifted himself to go get a coffee, Hannah saw the crushed red edges of his eyes and the shine on his face. He didn't even wipe the tears away; it was as if he wanted her to see them.

The door opens and her mother leans out, starts to say something, then stops. "Where'd they go?" she demands.

"He's gone," Hannah says quietly.

"What?"

"Gone, he's gone."

"What do you mean?" Hannah doesn't answer. "What do you *mean*, he's gone?"

The wind is picking up, moving the flaps on his boxes. Behind her, Hannah hears a shrivelled yellow apple drop to the grass.

# Do the
# Celine
# Thing

The five of us are in a car on Highway 40 coming back into town in the dark. "Tutti Frutti" is on the radio, neckties and pumps all over the dashboard with the tissue boxes, and empty Naya water bottles. Alice and Joaquin and me in the back seat, pounding our hands against the roof in time. Chris at the wheel yelling: "a wop bop a looba a wop bam boom." Bill with his eyes closed, his head whipping back and forth. The city passes under us like a galaxy.

My job is the easiest. I have the advanced class, all men. The first day I taught them the word "foreplay." Since then they take me to the warehouse catwalk during every break and fight over who will give me a cigarette.

Sometimes Joaquin comes to the catwalk with his class. He doesn't smoke; he might break a KitKat and pass it around. The students talk in French, and Joaquin and I lean over the railing and stare into the shelves below, the cardboard boxes with the tape on them tidy and brown. The concrete floor is cold until I toss my still-glowing cigarette butt down onto it.

₹℣

Every afternoon, Chris and Bill pick us up at Sherbrooke metro at four. They drop us back at our houses at eight. For the first two months it was a blast, but now we're getting tired, we complain about the snacks in the company cafeteria machines – chocolate and chips only – and about the reek of chlorine in the water from the fountains. Sometimes Joaquin brings apples for the ride home. We toss the cores out the window and make a wish with each one.

Alice is in charge of having a new dirty joke every night, and we make her save it for the stretch of the Metropolitain where we're almost home but stuck in traffic. Alice has lipstick on her perfect teeth, a grey-green smudge in the flickering roadlights, and the joke goes like this.

A guy walks into a bar and says to the bartender: I've invented this new thing. He pokes the palm of his hand seven times with his fingertip and holds his hand up to the side of his face. Hello? Mabel? Yeah, just running a test. I'll be home at seven. The bartender says, No way. Let me try that. The guy says, Yeah, okay, but hold on, I have to go do something. He goes into the bathroom. The bartender waits forty-five minutes and the guy doesn't come out, so he goes to the bathroom and knocks on the door. Yeah, it's okay, just hold on, the guy says. The bartender goes back to the bar and waits another half hour and the guy still doesn't come out. So he goes and opens the bathroom door. The guy's standing there with his hands pressed against the wall and a roll of toilet paper hanging out of his ass. The bartender says, What the fuck are you doing? And the guy says, Hang on, I won't be long. I'm just receiving a fax.

In the back seat, I sit in the middle because my legs are the shortest. Everyone but me has these long pony legs, Alice's smooth and unmarked. In September she came in little skirts and no pantyhose, not a stretchmark or spider vein in sight. She and I smoke Gauloises and blow blue at the back of Chris' head. Alice rolls her window down a crack and we let the wind take the ashes away.

Sometimes Chris makes Bill sing for us. Bill doesn't talk much; I can't imagine how he entertains his class for two hours. Chris prods him: "Come on, honey, do the Celine thing." Bill's grin is reflected in his window, flashing with the lights from the apartment buildings on the side of the highway. Finally he croons: "For I am your lady. . . ."

I start to join in. Alice and Joaquin lean forward, away from me and toward Bill.

☙

My men are restless, complaining about two hours of class a day, at supper time. I tell them Alice's fax joke and they toss their pencils into the air with joy.

We spend half an hour each evening planning our goodbye party, a trip to a pool hall in Laval. Someone's girlfriend is in Joaquin's class; they want to come along. I think of Joaquin in a pool hall with his tweed pants and shiny shoes. Then word travels, and we're all going, Alice and Chris and Bill too.

I pass by the door of Alice's class. Ashtrays are spread about – we aren't supposed to smoke anywhere except the warehouse. They're sitting around the table as though it's a dinner party; I never sit down in my class. She's laughing. She has all this golden hair, eyes like mud puddles. I get to the bathroom and close the door, lean against it with my hands behind my back, close my eyes.

There are places where I rule, but people like Alice rule everywhere.

When I get back to class one of them tells me this one. I

always say no Newfie jokes, but they never listen. A Newfie is driving along singing, "Bonne Fête à Moi, Bonne Fête à Moi." A UFO passes overhead and sucks up part of his brain. So he starts singing, "Bonne Fête, Bonne Fête, Bonne Fête." The UFO passes again and takes some more of his brain. He continues driving and now he's singing, "Bonne, Bonne, Bonne, Bonne." Finally the UFO passes one last time and takes all of his brain. And so he drives along singing, "Happy Birthday to You, Happy Birthday to You...."

I tell this joke when we're pulling out of the parking lot. Everyone crows, but then the laughter dissolves into the hot air from the vents. Alice looks out the window as though she thinks she might as well get out now.

⟳

There are thirty-five students and five of us. We take all the tables on the little mezzanine and order burgers with chili and pickles. The students insist on buying for the teachers. Every time we take a sip of beer, they fill our glasses until foam quivers like cloud.

Alice and Chris and Bill are strong drinkers. Joaquin and I are quickly drunk. My students say it's time to play pool. I've told them over and over that I'm the worst pool player they've ever met, and this seems to please them. Joaquin gets up to follow us, so his students come too.

One of my men shows me how to hold my cue, then takes it away to draw lines among the balls. Joaquin is sitting on a stool near the bar behind me. I wander away in the middle of the game, stand very close to him, his knee – in jeans tonight – almost between my legs. His glasses are foggy. He stares at me without expression. I suddenly feel nauseous.

I scuffle to the bathroom and stare at myself in the mirror while I wait for someone to finish in the stall. The light is greenish; I look like a mushroom covered in dust. Alice comes out of the stall and watches my mirrored face over my shoulder. Even she is ugly in here, skinny with hair flat yellow like piss on snow. "I was just receiving a fax," she says.

Her voice is sick with liquor. We giggle at the mirror, our cheeks pressed, her lipstick smudging me, her breath sour.

The Metropolitain passes under us like water. I'm thinking that if we concentrate, we can help Chris keep the car on the road. Then Bill starts singing. When I get home I won't remember the song. We all sing, but he sings the best.

# What Might Have Been Rain

# I
# OVERTURE

The essential thing is to remember, and I don't. I don't remember if there were houses along that road, or shrouds of palm and bamboo, or a domino chain of *warungs* and little shops selling sarongs and jute handbags. There must have been houses, because there were children, but they were all wearing little skirts the colour of burgundy wine, and white blouses, so maybe there was a school, and no houses.

Remembering is the thing, and what I remember, what I've been remembering since I left Japan, is Grace and the way Grace looked the last time, with her long angular legs and her cropped golden hair and the unrecognition that stretched all the way across the airport. Grace took the hand of some man and disappeared.

That was a few years ago. In airports I always think of Grace now. I thought of her in Kansai, imagined her going up and down in the glass elevator or standing in line at the money-changer. Of Grace in Denpasar, sitting on the next bench in the

103

blinding afternoon, with the line of taxi stands just visible over her shoulder. When there were no more airports, Grace didn't stop.

(The presence of god in the motorcycles:

Whole families ride together, the woman sidesaddle on the back with ankles crossed and feet held carefully, a little boy between his father's legs, a baby on the mother's lap. The streets spit dust.)

Now: in an excessively air-conditioned restaurant in Little India in Singapore. Singapore: it's as if someone took a cloth and a pail of warm soapy water and scrubbed the city briskly down, then rinsed it with a hose and dried it with a soft cloth. The damp doesn't stay after the torrential rains.


# II
# GREGORY

The first thing in Indonesia was Gregory; even before Indonesia there was Gregory. We went to Ubud first of all. Gregory was white and travel-sick the whole way, but when we disembarked he insisted on searching for the perfect room. This took as long as the journey from Denpasar. The balcony projected into the coconuts and bougainvillea, and there were geckos on the walls. We tied up the army-green mosquito net with some white raffia string. Then I went to call Johanna.

Some of the things I can say about Johanna are: she has a face, and a tongue, and hands, and vowels all confused. Grace's vowels were like that, and her legs were like Johanna's too, from what I can remember.

Gregory waited. I didn't know him well. I wondered if all I knew of him was something he'd made up. I thought that he was inventing this patience. There were hard, uncomplaining lines in his face.

### THE FACE

The face is the surface of the body, giving
birth to utterance, carnal, the seat of
subjecthood, multisurfaced, coloured in
danger, an unmistakable witness. The face
is cultivated and produced in families, in
the schoolyard, all alone in the dark. The
face is transformed by silence. Anything
that passes through it must traverse
the body first. The face is excavable,
palpable. Its most significant topography
is the instructions that remain eternally
inscribed.

### THE TONGUE

The tongue is an extension of the face. The
tongue is that place where there is at first
no language. The face cannot always take
in the tongue. The tongue grows words
on its surface. It is a shape made of flesh.
The tongue transgresses. It is drenched,
numbed, linked. It sometimes rebels
against what has been engraved. It is not
transformed by silence. It sometimes falls,
and sometimes is shoved, into cracked
spaces.

### THE HAND

The hand, wherein there is always
language, is an extension of the face.
Anything that passes through the hand
must traverse the body first. The hand
is a shape made of bones, giving birth
to utterance. It rips out stitches. It sees

through membranes. It contains entrails
and adrenaline. In silence, it rests.

I made this trip mostly because I was in love with Gregory.
Johanna was simply an enticement, a puzzle. Indonesia was
just a backdrop, and still is, even in retrospect. Indonesia isn't
a character in this story. Singapore might be, if only because
it refuses, in all its oppressive comfort and cleanliness, to be
silenced.

(The presence of god in the geckos:

They move very quickly. I once owned a jigsaw puzzle of
which each piece looked like a gecko, and each piece fitted to
each other piece in seven or eight different ways so the only clue
was colour.)

Later, Gregory was still white and ill, which was exactly
what was necessary.


# III
# JOHANNA

Before we ran away to Lovina, Johanna and I went to visit the
*candi* at Gunung Kawi. We had to walk down many steps and
cross a river. As we were going down, three girls were coming
up. They were younger than us, but not much younger, maybe
nineteen or twenty, and they were all brown and thin and their
faces were brazen, without apology. The first girl had her arm
around the waist of the second girl who was holding the hand
of the third girl. They were wearing print cotton dresses well
above their knees, one blue, one green, one lavender, all with
white, all faded. They were holding towels, and one had a basin.
They looked at us boldly and without curiosity or concern, then
turned to follow some steps down to the waterfall. We saw them
begin to take off their dresses.

That night, Gregory's blackish eyes were cold, as he once told me they used to be all the time. I thought it might be because I didn't keep vigil at his bed that day as he nursed his traveler's diarrhea. He said, "I asked you to come with me so that I could spend this time with you. I don't think you came here to spend this time with me."

I did, of course, go there to spend this time with him, because I knew it was the only way to make myself understand. What I wanted to understand is no longer clear to me, but at that time, still warm from the sun over Gunung Kawi, it seemed obvious. I'd come there to be with Gregory, but Gregory was now cranky and hadn't seen those girls by the waterfall. I'd gone there to have a realization about Gregory, and that evening I decided to have it.

(The presence of God with a capital G in the silver bracelets:

I didn't go to Kota Gede to buy them. I bought them from the shopping mall on Jalan Malioboro, at the little kiosk next to the California Fried Chicken restaurant. One bracelet is triangular, the other rectangular. All the corners are round. Together they cost me 48,000 rupiah, about 2,000 yen, about twenty-five Canadian dollars. The only thing that cost me more was my airplane ticket to Singapore.)

On the beach in Lovina, after we ran away, Johanna and I met two little girls about ten years old who wanted to sell us necklaces made of beads and shells. At first we said no several times, but they pouted and wouldn't go away, so we chose a few and bargained with them to see them pout some more. They sat on our bench with us and played with my red hair and told us we were beautiful. One had a Canadian dollar coin and asked us to give her rupiah for it. We laughed and asked, didn't she want it as a souvenir? The stupidity of this didn't strike us until later.

This was after we ran away. After I decided one night not to go back to the room where Gregory was recovering from what might be dysentery, and got on a bus to Lovina with Johanna instead. Faces, tongues, hands, and so on, are not all the same.

The things I do not remember: whether we were coming from or going to, what came before and what came after and the distance between them; whether she screamed, cowered, or simply fell; whether it was still raining, or not.

I'm surprised, now, that Grace was everywhere with me when I arrived, even before I saw Johanna in Ubud. Maybe it was Johanna's voice on the phone, back in Japan where she was still safely far away and I hadn't taken into account what legs and vowels and other parts of the body can do to one's judgment.

There are two parts to my memory of Grace: one is Johanna, the other is Ilse. Johanna is the face, the tongue, the hands, and the legs. Ilse is the hair, the eyes, the cigarettes, and the legs. I don't know if Grace would ever push me into a patch of Indian gooseberry orchids as Ilse did, or hit a little Balinese schoolgirl with a jeep in what might have been rain, as Johanna did. I don't know much about Grace any more.

THE FACE

The face is an element of earth, inclusive, directly knowing the world. It yields to some and is penetrated by some. It merges hidden motives. It is the last part to be colonized. It is definite and external. It sustains itself. It barters. It contains a beginning and an end. It has a hole in the center containing fiery rocks, or a bird's nest, or a tablet. The heat that moves through the body sits in the face like the sun. The face is the outward or forward action. It is a sequence and a morass. It is not an idol. It is a glyph, a consort, and a harbinger.

### THE TONGUE

The tongue reaches out and encloses, like
a tree or rock walls. Like the tortoise, it
carries the world on its back. It contains
lots of earth. It circles. It has a craft, and
requires apprenticeship. It can weave
tapestry and string beads. It is a movement
of the personality. It regenerates cells.
It can be a weapon or a wrench. It is,
like an octopus, watery and receptive,
and glorious. It is tipped with different
symbols. It severs itself. It is not without
distinctive features. It is an intelligent
substance that can fashion the world as
dead, alive, or a table to hold spoils. It
contains marrow.

### THE HAND

The hand is resplendent. It embodies all
quests. It is the opening of the voice. It
can ask water to flow from the ground
for our use. The hand is the place in us
that survives. It is a cupule, like a breast
mark found in stone. It believes in what
is holy and known in one's cells, not one
or the other. The hand is sometimes a
salamander and sometimes a lion. The
hand has roots in the wrist. The hand
knows the way to make fire: kindling;
harnessing; friction. The hand knows
the power of creating systems. It slices. It
is sometimes false. The hand stings and
puffs with small, contained explosions. It
is sometimes a gryphon and sometimes

a phoenix. The hand has a chronology
and a belly. It can make flour, porridge,
amaranth, and sanctuary. It is sometimes
a granary, sometimes moon-mad, and
sometimes a starfish.

All these objects are functional.

(The presence of god in the orchids:

The Indian gooseberry, or *melaka*, is a small, cream-coloured orchid with a purple heart and purple speckles like rain. There are large clumps of them around the steps leading to the VIP section of the Singapore Orchid Garden. Ilse knocked me into one of those clumps just hours ago, after I childishly called her an Aryan whore because she was planning to abscond to Malaysia with my girlfriend. If she had to knock me into anything, I'm glad it was those. I hope there are still some petals clinging to my hair as I sit here shivering from artificial cold while outside the sun braises Little India.)

In Lovina, Johanna struck an eight-year-old schoolgirl with our rented jeep. It wasn't Johanna's fault. We were careening in the style of any self-respecting Indonesian driver, and the child saw us – and we saw ourselves register on her small, uncertain face – before she darted out into the road. What made her think she could reach the other side before we reached her is unclear. We didn't kill her, and this is all I remember.

Johanna was simply an echo of Grace, except for her long straight black hair like a Japanese woman's but nothing like Grace's; her freckled slim nose nothing like Grace's; with her eyes all warm amber nothing like Grace's. Gregory knew, somehow, and that was why he wanted to leave Johanna behind, leave her as long as possible; every time I said Johanna's name something in his mottled face sealed over. He doesn't know her, but he knows some things about me. I'm sitting here in this ridiculously cold restaurant in Singapore's Little India, unable to eat my vegetables vindaloo because I'm not nearly as sturdy (of stomach, of palate, of will) as I'd like to believe, and I miss the thin stiff muscles on Gregory's arms and the tension in the smile he comes by most easily. I'm wondering if there's any way I could have stayed with him in Ubud. And there is: if I'd known Johanna was on her way to something, I might not have come.

But chances are, I would've come. I knew she was on her way to something when we hit that little girl. That was why we couldn't stay. As soon as I saw Ilse, standing in that huge mudyard before the ferryboat buying a chocolate ice cream, I knew that Johanna was on her way to something.

## IV
## ILSE

Ilse took a bite before she saw us. When she met Johanna's eyes she smiled, and the ice cream smudged her chin. She dropped the whole thing into a nearby pail and came toward us.

There are two parts to my memory of Grace. Ilse is the wheat-coloured hair, the pale eyes, and the legs. And the cigarettes. Without wiping the sticky brown smudge (I suspect she wanted it there as I want the orchid petals stuck in my red hair), she pulled a Gudang Garam *kretek* out of the air and lit it, wafting toward us with the scent of cloves.

Gregory once gave me a packet of *kretek* cigarettes. He bought them at a specialty tobacco shop in Osaka. I'd told him that I used to buy them for myself in Montreal. Gregory didn't like me to smoke, but he liked the smell and the expressions on my face that Indonesian clove cigarettes created. I was remembering what *kretek* cigarettes did to Grace and her face.

THE FACE

The face lives the most lives the quickest.
We can shave a little bit off and fix it while
we sleep. The face is rife with multiple
negatives and erroneous notions. We
sharpen the face with the body.

THE TONGUE

The tongue circumscribes and pervades,
distorts and lessens.

THE HAND

The hand unearths.

They were going to Malaysia, Johanna explained. Yogyakarta, Jakarta, Singapore, Malaysia. Johanna didn't plan to return to Japan at all. There was nothing to do but go with them. If I took the jeep back, as Johanna suggested, somebody would surely identify it. "But we didn't kill her," I said. "Why don't we just go back and tell somebody? Why didn't we just stop?"

It was Ilse who made me understand, not that she spoke. Looks were exchanged. I realized that Ilse had been waiting here all along. She hadn't come to help Johanna escape from a crime; Johanna hadn't called her while I was in the gas-station toilet and asked her to rescue her because something had gone terribly wrong. Ilse had known to come here all along, because Johanna had been escaping since I grasped at her through the telephone in Ubud, maybe since before that, and we hadn't stopped on that road

(where there were rice fields, I remember now, and it wasn't raining)

because Johanna hadn't wanted Ilse to get on this boat without her.

(She moved after, she jumped even, and ran. Out of the

way, so that we could keep going, so that there was no reason to stop.)

Now, in Singapore, I'm getting ready to go home.

## V
## GRACE

I always think of Grace in airports, although she never saw me in one.

The essential thing is to remember Grace's face, which looked like this: she had two eyes, which were pale with a suspicion of green like the water at Lovina Beach; and she had a big, turned-up nose; and she was somewhere between vanilla-ice cream-coloured and brandy-coloured; and her teeth were strong and even; and she often wore her sunshine-coloured hair in a ponytail that sprouted directly from her scalp, until she cut it all off so that she would look more like a boy.

(The presence of god in airports:)

In Kansai there was a glass elevator going up and down, and I saw Grace in it. In Bangkok there was a pharmacy which sold Tiger Balm, and as I was spending my sixty baht I saw Grace across the blue plastic waiting room, cudgeling something on a game machine with a big plastic bat, and laughing. In Denpasar there were taxi stands, and Grace was sitting there in the sun.

We took the boat to Yogyakarta and found a hotel with a balcony. I went to the air-conditioned shopping mall on Jalan Malioboro and bought a banana split with durian ice cream, which I couldn't finish, but I sat at the table with smudges on my face for a while. Then I went to the kiosk, next to California Fried Chicken, where there was silver from Kota Gede, and bought two silver bracelets, one triangular, one rectangular.

They offered to let me share the bed.

The essential thing to remember is that when Grace and

I were seventeen her mother discovered us on the divan in the attic and called my mother to say that she never wanted to see me in her house again. Grace didn't cry and she didn't get angry. She shrugged and lit one of those sweet-smelling cigarettes, and sometimes she returned my phone calls, but she never said very much. She'd been my best friend since we were seven.

After that, even after I stopped believing I would die from her, boys were safer.

From Yogya to Jakarta, and all the time I was thinking of Gregory's polished eyes and thinking that I should really be leaving now – the exact frame of time escaped me, dates had become fluid – and watching their faces. Their faces were very careful.

They almost made it to Singapore without me, and I almost let them, but I didn't want this whole story to be about Indonesia, I didn't want Johanna to end with nothing but Indonesia, and so I had to buy an airplane ticket with money I didn't have, and I had to see one more airport. This time Grace was on the other side of the Plexiglas while we sat in the Transfer Passengers Lounge. She was there not looking at me, her mouth too high for the little intercom – I'd forgotten she was tall – and it became apparent that I was going to Singapore but she was staying here, and that was why I'd have to speak to her through a window if I were to speak to her at all. I had to stand on the stairs in the hostel and watch Johanna with the face, tongue, hands, and legs and Ilse with the hair, eyes, legs, and one perfumy cigarette ask for a double room and . . . and look at me all questions, as if to say, you can visit if you like. And I thought, I'll go home tomorrow, I'll go back to where I come from tomorrow, and I followed them.

I wanted to find Grace in the sum of their parts. But Grace was still back where I came from.

When I woke up I was in the middle, and each of them looked so long and barely three-dimensional that it was easy to just pick up my things and go out into the rain.

THE FACE

The essential thing is to remember the
face, until you can bear to leave it where it
was.

## VI
## EPILOGUE

I'm not sure that it was Ilse who pushed me into the patch of
Indian gooseberry. She had Grace's hair, the colour of a Canadian
one-dollar coin, and Grace's eyes, a bit sleepy and hinted with
green like durian ice cream, and Grace's legs, like Johanna's legs,
the legs I always wanted to have, and she was holding a cigarette
that smelled like Indonesia.

# Wall of
# Weeds

On the boat to Samosir Island, I meet a man and a woman from India, a brother and sister named Rajinder and Kulvinder. They're visiting their uncle, the owner of a hotel called "Tondi." Rajinder is long-haired and gazelle-like; his nails are painted coral pink. He crosses his thin legs primly under his grey-and-rose checkered sarong as he leans forward to ask me questions. He tells me he studied in Toronto, and plans to go back as soon as he can blackmail the money out of his affluent father in the Punjab. Kulvinder, also skinny, looks much older than him, perhaps around forty, with ornate glasses, and a blanket to protect her from the wind coming off one of the deepest lakes in the world. She says nothing during the hour-long journey, and when we reach Tondi, she climbs off the boat and walks away without looking at me.

Rajinder leads me by the hand to his uncle, who takes me down a tiny stone path on the lakefront to bungalow number five.

༖

I leave the curtains open and fall asleep to the sound of the waves tumbling over one another. Then I wake up, startled, to silence in the blackness. Everything has stopped moving.

Later I wake up again, and the sun is coming rising; I can see light on the surface of the still lake. I lie and watch the solid water out the window, wondering what would happen if I tried to swim in it.

A man moves across the skin of the lake in his wooden canoe, tossing a net, bit by bit, behind him. He takes a pole from the bottom of the boat and, with it, slaps the water. I feel the shivers spread all the way to my bed.

I stand and go to the window.

Kulvinder, in a lavender swimsuit, stands thigh-deep in the water, looking out, away from me. She walks a few steps and then sinks up to her neck. She starts moving away quickly, a black head intent upon the other shore.

In the afternoon the rains come.

"I came because I'm pregnant," I tell Rajinder.

I ask Kulvinder about the lake. She smiles, nudging her glasses up on her face. "For two months I've been swimming every day," she says. "I haven't been sick, and I haven't seen anything more threatening than seaweed. But you should go in the morning, because later, there are winds."

The next morning when the sun is rising, the lake is cold on my ankles, and under my feet, clay-like and slimy. I start walking, watching the line of waterweeds come closer and closer. When I'm up to my armpits, the green tentacles reach toward me, and I contract.

I stand there, breathing. I try to touch one of the feathery fingers moving under the water, but I can't; my hand won't allow me. I hold my head up, take a breath, and raise my feet from the clay. I paddle blindly. The molestation lasts only a moment, and then the lake opens up under me, glass-green.

I have no idea where the bottom is.

Rowan's eyes are empty. He fixes them on things, on me, as though he's been in a state of epiphany for so long that it no longer surprises him. At our Christmas dinner, he and Kulvinder begin to discuss the inadequacies of feminism in addressing the problem of the abused male, and I stop listening.

Dinner is curried tofu, mashed potatoes, salad, eggs, rice, and papaya for dessert. Rajinder and I make eggnog. There's only powdered milk, but there's also fresh nutmeg that we grate to a pulp. Everyone says politely that it's delicious.

After dinner we pile wood on the beach to make a fire, and I hear Rowan ask Kulvinder if she wants to go for a walk.

The next morning, Rowan and Kulvinder are nowhere to be found. All Rowan's things are gone, but everything in Rajinder's room is exactly as Kulvinder left it. The police are called; when they eventually arrive, they are slow-spoken and amused.

Rajinder and I go for a swim in the afternoon. The water is still calm. I take the rubber inner tube from the beach so I can float over the weeds and get to the depth of things, where the ripples are no stronger than those in a waterbed.

Rajinder paddles around me among the thin clouds of white lakeflies, his black hair floating in a pool around his face, his little bum in its tiny white bikini occasionally showing itself above the surface. I can see he's trying to immerse himself in something other than his concern. I'm lying on my back on top of black inflated rubber, mildly excited at the intrigue. Then I hear the wind coming.

A wave, small but strong and unexpected, tips me into the water. When my head comes up I hear a sort of hissing, a sort of rushing, and I feel it too, moving me, knocking me against the waiting wall of weeds. I start to tremble, sending out a different kind of ripple.

The inner tube has moved away, just out of my reach. Rajinder has gone after it and I'm here in the weeds and they're wrapping themselves around me very, very gently as if to say *don't be scared.* I don't know whether to kick or to float or to let them do what they have to. The waves are pushing me into the weeds, like rain that makes you seek shelter deeper and deeper in the forest.

As I stay there, held upright by the hands of the weeds, I look out and along, toward the beach. Kulvinder is held upright, just barely upright, by something not visible, at the edge of the water. There's blood on her, and torn clothes, and behind me her brother has forgotten about me and my inner tube and isn't leaving it up to the waves to bring him ashore.

Kulvinder goes home to the Punjab and Rajinder takes me to Thailand. I'm standing on the ocean, supported by the floor of this fishing village, a floor made of planks a few metres above the water. Rajinder and I have been walking in circles around this boardwalk community, this town made of salt water and wood, but now we're standing, and he has one hand on my belly and is asking me why I brought this baby to the tropics. A young barefoot woman with a sun-orange sarong wrapped above her breasts steps between us and thrusts a white-faced gibbon into my arms.

"You want photo?" she asks.

## Wall of Weeds

The gibbon grasps my T-shirt and looks up at me, its black-rimmed eyes huge holes in its white face. I place a hand gently on its head. It's soft, like black feathers on a baby chicken. The gibbon pulls itself closer to me and presses its nose into my breast.

"You want photo?" the woman repeats irritably.

I shake my head, and my bowels clench. I pull my shirt from the gibbon's hands and trot back to the pier, where someone directs me to a toilet. The toilets in Thailand are cleaner than those in Indonesia, but they don't always smell good, and they're designed in such a way that it's easy to tell when your stool is full of mucus and blood.

They bundle Rajinder and me back into the longboat and back to Phuket. Rajinder takes me to the hospital, and when we get there, I'm bleeding in the place where the baby would have been. The doctor confirms that I was pregnant but that I'm not any longer, and that I should be ashamed of having undertaken this journey in my condition, and that I have bacillary dysentery. He gives me pocketfuls of pills and sends me away.

Rajinder takes me to the hotel and puts me to bed, brings me a papaya and makes me chew the seeds, which burn my tongue like curry powder, and mixes rehydration salts into a bottle of water. Then he leaves me alone to read the *Bangkok Post*. My fever moves the words around before me like weeds in a hot lake.

ༀ

The fever subsides after two days, and Rajinder takes me swimming with the glowing green fish at Coral Island. I stay near the shore, where the water is clearest, and tell him I don't want a snorkel mask. He gets me one anyway, and he keeps moving farther and farther out, toward the place where there is no shore, and I keep following him, and nothing touches me, nothing tries to take me down.

121

# Mordecai

We make love in the hotel bed that afternoon, the fluffy four-poster with the tough nubby linen sheets. I love the ways our bodies are the same, his tall and broad and mine small and round, but both blonde and white, with precise pockets of softness and dark wiriness. Both of us loud and furious.

We've learned what not to touch with what, and when. We've had a year to learn a lot about danger, about what's worth it and what's not. I'm astonished by his willingness, his desire, to do this. To risk everything. I don't know if I'd be willing, if I were him. I tell myself I would.

Afterwards we lie still, his face pressed against my neck, his hands moving over the outside surfaces: the small of my back, the pliable ripples and stretch scars of my buttocks and the backs of my thighs. The transparent curtains look out on the swish and jar of a service station, and the noise and my gratitude are so loud that it's minutes before I realize that he's crying.

It's not certain that I'll die. I've said this to him before, many times, but it's never seemed to comfort him.

⇌

Joe grumbles as we wait for the elevator. "Why the desert? It's not a real desert, it can't be."

"There are rattlesnakes and cactuses. . . ."

"Cacti, Lisa."

"Shut up. Cactuses and antelope brush and sand. It's a desert."

"Why the desert?" He jabs the elevator button a few more times. "Why not a walk around Stanley Park? Why not the Maya Canyon?"

"We can go to the Maya Canyon if you want. It's not far from there." The elevator opens.

My mother and the car are waiting for us in front of the hotel. I make introductions. Joe shakes her hand heartily; when he lets go, Pat stares at her hand as though she no longer recognizes it. I'm tempted to give her a warning look, but I know this won't help.

I let Joe sit in the front because of his long legs and because it frees me to stare out the window undisturbed. Pat doesn't look altogether happy about this arrangement, but for the first hundred kilometres or so, Joe doesn't say much, and this seems to relax her. The road to Hope is fast and wide, and passes by in a blur of trees and houses and tumbling mountains. My eyes are throbbing like sore muscles.

"How do you like Vancouver, Joe?" Pat is asking.

Joe shrugs. "I've never really liked Vancouver." He's bellowing. I specifically told him not to bellow at her. He may be bellowing on purpose, or he may not be able to help himself. "All this ecstasy about the landscape: the mountains! the trees! oh my god, the ocean! Means little to me, frankly. People here work too much, and complain about the weather all the time; if they ever lived in Montreal, they'd shut up about it."

"I love the weather here." Pat's face, in the rearview mirror, is hard.

"No one walks to work," Joe continues. He has reigned his voice in a little. "Then they spend their weekends killing themselves trekking up mountains. Can't get a real bagel anywhere, and people seem to think bubble tea is supposed to compensate. Who ever came up with bubble tea? It's disgusting."

"The Vietnamese, I think it was," says Pat.

"Well, they should have kept it to themselves. I like the fondness for biking. I can appreciate that. But sushi. Lisa keeps going on about sushi." Joe's voice is rising again. "Who cares? Why not just chew on a raw trout? You can get those anywhere. The only decent coffee is at Starbucks, and I can't condone Starbucks. Can't find a microbrewed beer I like." He leans his head back against the headrest and sighs. "No, Vancouver is not the place for me."

There's a pause.

"But . . . " he turns his blue eyes and leans toward her slightly, bumping her hand on the gearshift, " . . . there must be an up side, as you've decided to live here."

Pat's face in the mirror is motionless except her lips. "I enjoy the trees! the mountains! as you put it."

"Yes," says Joe, nodding and watching her face eagerly, "exactly. If that's important for you, this is the place to be."

"And I do walk to work, just about every day. It's not as lively and European-market-like as Montreal, but the cherry trees are nice."

"Yes," says Joe, tipping his head back against the headrest, his eyes still on Pat, "I hadn't thought of the cherry trees."

"And I like bubble tea."

"Me too," I say, leaning forward between the seats. "Red bean."

"From that coffee shop on Pender." Pat grins at me in the mirror.

"Yum."

"All right, this I cannot concede," Joe tells the roof. "Bubble tea is vile. If you want beverage, I say, get beverage. If you want pudding, have pudding. Do not confuse me with blobs. It's not a drink. It's…a marine ecosystem." Pat chuckles at this. "I will tell you, though: I like the SkyTrain. It must be nice to live in a place where the metro doesn't need to be underground. There is nothing more depressing than crawling into a hole to get somewhere."

"If only there were more lines," Pat sighs. "I miss that about Montreal. All the lines."

"Granted," Joe agrees, nodding at the roof. "There's a lot to be said for more lines."

ᴎᐱ

We stop for coffee at a hippyish little place next to a gas station – what is this doing here, I wonder – and then drive to the Hope Slide so Pat can take some pictures. "In the sixties," Pat explains, "an earthquake made the whole mountain topple onto the highway. Four people died; two of them are still buried in there somewhere. They had to build a new road. This road."

It just looks like a big quarry to me, not so much a disaster as a decision. It reminds me of the abandoned quarry I used to go to with friends when I was a teenager, so we could climb around in the dark and feel like adventurers, so we could drink beer someone's older brother bought us at the corner store. Such a faraway place, such a long-ago time; that's how it feels, although it's not so long ago really, barely more than ten years. Even Montreal, where I live now, where I was just a couple of weeks ago, seems far away, centuries past. I can hardly remember the small town I grew up in or the person I was when I lived there. I can hardly remember my father, although I saw him less than two years ago. I hardly remembered my mother until I got here.

Nothing that happened to me before Joe seems real. I feel like scraps of a once-offending photo that I'm trying to put back together. I watch myself emerging, a Scotch-tape-scarred approximation of the original.

Pat has us stand at the lookout so she can get a shot of us in front of the landslide. Then she asks Joe to step aside so she can take a picture of me alone. No, I think. You're not allowed to picture me without him any more. The coffee rises in my throat, and I sit down hard on the side of the railing and put my head in my hands. I sit and breathe for a while, and finally spit onto the gravel.

When I look up, Joe and Pat are standing on either side of me. Joe is looking out toward the Hope Slide as though waiting for it to do something. Pat sits down on the railing next to me and watches my face intently. I find this intrusive, and turn my face away. Joe looks down at the two of us. He's biting his lips together, and his eyes are wet and burning like the dull blue of brandy touched by flame.

⌇

It's dark when we reach the campsite. Joe and Pat set up the tents. I say I'm going to the washroom, and wander down to the lake. Odd, I think. A lake in the desert.

I slept most of the way from Hope, stretched across the back seat like a dog rug, but I'm still worn through and brittle with fatigue. I take off my shoes and roll up my cuffs, step down to the waterline, walk out and find that even after a few metres, the water doesn't rise above my ankles. I walk a little further, then some more, pull my trousers above my knees and continue. I look back at the shore, winking at me with camp stoves and the lights along the main road. No fires allowed here, the brochure warned, but I can see one further down the beach, maybe in the communal pit.

I dip my hands in the water and wipe them over my face, smooth my hair down. Under my feet, the rocks have turned to soft sand. The lake is lapping, wetting the edges of my cuffs. The lakefront campsites are very close to the shore, and I can hear quiet voices calling back and forth, asking for tent pegs and packs of cards and another bag of chips.

Tomorrow I want to ride a horse, and see a rattlesnake, and get my hair full of sand. I want to swim all the way across the lake. I want to get stuck with a cactus and I want. . . .

I turn toward the shore again and see a tall, broad man, his hair shaggy and yellow like a golden retriever's, standing in the shadow of the campsite trees. I take a step closer, and then another. He's standing still, not gesturing for me to come to him, just watching and waiting. But as I wade toward him, and the shore, I see that it isn't Joe at all. It isn't anyone. It seems to have been the light, reflecting through the trees in a peculiar fashion. It isn't Joe at all, and yet I absolutely, unquestioningly, believed that it was.

⮂

We make love in our tent in silence. It's pitch black. When he lets go a gasp, I fumble through the dark to find his lips and press them with my fingers. I feel his nod under my hand, and then slide the hand down to grasp him like a talisman; against his chest I hear the silent groan quicken his heart. He plunges his fingers into me brutally, as though in punishment, and I come in a heartbreaking flash, sinking my teeth into the tender flesh under his arm.

Afterwards, he presses his breath, as it cools, against my eyes, my neck, the stretching skin at the top of my breasts.

"Joe?"

"Yes, my love."

"What if I don't die? What will you do then?"

The words shiver in the cold desert air. How many times do I think I can do this? Can I keep expecting him not to break because he is so large?

"You will die, darling," he whispers. "We all will."

For a long time I don't believe he's asleep. Even my nearsighted eyes can see the blackness inside the tent very clearly. I hear a rustle from Pat's tent, as though she isn't sleeping either. But it could be rattlesnakes, or the sound of desert plants growing.

彡

In the morning I crawl out of the tent, hair standing up, eyes bleary with dry sleep. A black straining horse gallops past the campsite, with a shirtless brown boy with no shoes on its bare back. I rub my face and look again. They head toward the campground shop, then out of sight. I put my head into the tent to reach over Joe for my toothbrush, and when I straighten up, the horse, whinnying and tossing its head, is pounding back in the other direction, alone. A moment later the brown boy races past, sweating. He sees me, and raises a hand in sheepish greeting. Then he disappears.

I laugh so uncontrollably that I have to sit on the ground, and Joe, still half asleep, sticks his head out of the tent to see what the commotion is about.

Pat and I go to the stable to ask for a horse ride while Joe stays behind to make breakfast. On the way, Pat puts a hand on my arm, and we stop in the middle of the dirt road and look at one another. My heart sinks deep in my lungs, the way it always does now when I know my mother wants to tell me something important.

"He's very brave," she says. "But don't you worry? How would you feel if he got it too?"

There is, of course, no answer. After a moment of looking at my face, her hand drops from my arm. "I'm sorry," she whispers. We walk the rest of the way to the stables in silence.

We stand around the pen until the shirtless barefoot rider from this morning calls my name; I climb over the fence and he leads me to a brown gelding with a white spotted rump like a speckled egg. He helps me into the saddle. I grin at him, but his smile is merely polite.

"This morning," I ask, "did the horse throw you off?"

He laughs, showing broken teeth. "Hell, no. I've never been thrown in my life. I left him by the store and some of the kids wanted to pet him. I told them not to spook him, but they ran at him and he bolted. Horses are like people. If a stranger runs at you, what do you do? You run the other way."

My horse's name is Mordecai. I think this is a wonderful name, and I ask the handsome brown horseman how a horse with such a name came to be among the Jokers and Banjos and Tramps. He shrugs. "I think we bought him from some Jewish guy and named it after him. It was before my time."

The riding party includes a pile of schoolchildren and their parents. A pudgy, broad-faced little girl, who whines in terror when they hoist her onto her horse, is wearing a T-shirt that says CHRIST WILL GIVE YOU THE ANSWER. Pat, sitting stiffly on a greyish horse named Paolo, glances at me, glances at the T-shirt, and rolls her eyes. She leans precariously from her saddle and whispers, "Promise me you will never move to the Okanagan."

I grin. "Your promises are too easy." Her face seems to whiten for a moment, but she forces a smile.

We start off in a train, Mordecai's nose to Paolo's tail, the horses clearly accustomed to the drill. The boy is at the head on his black horse (his "steed," I think, although I'm not sure what "steed" means), and another horsehand rides a shiny chestnut at the back. We trudge up onto the desert walk, the horses' hoofs slippery yet sure on the pliant sand.

I pat Mordecai's mane absently and the breeze moves the milky early light around us. Cliffs rise on one side, sand-pale and rock-grey, and on the other side is the valley where the town of Osoyoos waves with the distant movement of a sleepy morning. Pat's back ahead of me is stiff and worried, her hands on Paolo's reins rigid. I note this, and then forget about it, as I peer below Mordecai's feet at the cactuses – cacti, I correct myself, grimacing – and the movement of the sand.

The man at the rear gallops his horse off the trail and forward until he is just ahead of me and calls, "There he is, can you all see?" He has a long stick in his hand and is poking around in the brush. As I approach, he points to the ground with his stick, and says, "Look, look, there you are." A dark golden snake slithers to the base of the bush closest to Mordecai, curls around itself and lifts its nose into the air. Its black jewel eyes are looking straight at me. I hear a faint, beady rattle. Then the snake moves off, away from the trail, and the horses plod on their way.

When I look up, Pat is staring around at me and grinning, her eyes wide like a little girl's. "Did you see?"

I nod. "Yes, Mom. Did you?

Pat nods, breathless. "Yes. Yes, I did."

We stop at the top of the incline, over the valley, so the horsehands can trot around and take pictures with the schoolchildren's cameras. They swerve and dart like snakes themselves, occasionally barking, "Stand, José!" or, "Banjo, you'll get lunch when you get back. Don't let him eat on the trail, sweetheart."

We head around and down the trail, the girl in the Christ T-shirt moaning, "Oh, Mommy, my knees hurt, my knees hurt, are we almost there?" My knees hurt, too; I take my feet out of the stirrups to stretch my legs a little, then put them back in. The sun is brighter, and burning my face underneath the breeze. I think: I have seen that boy bareback on his black horse, galloping. I have seen that. And a rattlesnake, too.

We curl around the main road, and I think I might be ready to trot now, or even to gallop if I knew Mordecai was a good horse. Maybe I could learn to ride without a saddle, holding on with my knees, which would be better and stronger by then. I could live here in Osoyoos and see rattlesnakes every day. Then I realize I'm holding too tight to the reins. I let them go, and Mordecai leans forward and nips Paolo on his grey backside. Paolo rears up with a whinny, and Pat, whose feet are out of her stirrups, gives a truncated shriek, slides off the back of the saddle, knocks Mordecai's head, and tumbles onto the ground.

"Pull back on your reins!" cries the man on the chestnut horse, and everybody does, preventing the horses from rearing upon one another like a chain of dominoes. Mordecai is tossing his head and stamping. I pull back firmly and stroke his mane, murmuring, "It's okay, baby, it's okay." Finally he calms. I try to swing one leg over, but my sore knees buckle and give, and I twist one leg in the stirrup as I plunge to the ground.

Pat, lying on the ground near me covered in dust, is groaning and gasping and laughing all at once. "I'm okay, oh Christ, I'm okay. Oh, my tailbone. Lisa, Lisa baby, are you all right?"

"I don't know. Ow. I don't think so. Shit, my leg."

The shirtless boy is beside me, pulling my foot from where it remains hoisted in the stirrup. "All right, you're okay, we have to get you off the trail so we can get the horses out of the way." He puts an arm around me and pulls me up to my feet like a sack, as the rattlesnake man does the same for my mother. "Don't put any weight on that leg just yet. Christ, what a start to the day."

I laugh briefly. "Sorry to spoil your morning."

"Didn't mean it that way, miss. I was thinking of you."

We limp off the trail, and the rattlesnake man deposits Pat gently on the ground and runs back to lead the train of jittery horses back to the stable. Pat is still laughing, tears in her eyes. "Oh, Jesus. Lisa, Lisa, what happened to your leg?"

"My leg will be fine." The black horse boy slides me down to the ground and checks my ankle, my knee, my thigh with his hands.

"What are you trying to find, young man?" Pat demands, through her tears.

Then I start laughing too, a little hysterically.

The boy looks from me to Pat, his sunbrown face quizzical and exasperated. "I think you ladies are going to be all right. Do either of you want to see a doctor? Or both, maybe?"

As I gasp for breath, I look down the road toward the campsites.

The sun is starting to blaze; it will be a hot, clear day, a good day for swimming, now that I've hurt myself and can't go wandering through the desert putting my hands on the spines of cactuses – cacti – and picking the sage brush by the handfuls. I'm hungry. I wonder if Joe's finished the porridge, or if he's been sitting at the picnic table staring at something – the bright desert sky the colour of our eyes, or the people wandering back and forth with their RVs and children and golden retrievers – and making a decision, a small or a large one. Because the truth is – and I've known this all along, especially since we arrived here and he started complaining about the trees! the mountains! the bubble tea! – that decisions like "Yes," like "Stay," are never really made, never really decided; only decisions like "No" and "Go" and "Save yourself" amount to anything that is sure to last.

He has probably finished the porridge.

If I am really hurt – and I'm fairly sure I'm not, just a twist of the knee maybe, nothing a bit of ice won't fix – the only person who will be of any help in this brief moment on the desert sand won't be Joe, who isn't here, who's back at the campsite making porridge; nor my mother, who still can't stop laughing although I've taken a deep breath and fallen silent. The only one who can help me with this ailment, right now, on this morning, under this sun, is this young person with no shirt and no shoes. Tomorrow something else may go wrong, and I will have to seek help in entirely different quarters. My mother can drive me to the hospital, and Joe can hold my hand, but in the end, those things are not what is really needed.

There will come a day when nothing, and nobody, can help. But as Joe says, that's true for everyone.

If I concentrate, I can almost imagine a tall, heavy figure, with hair like a golden retriever's, running along the road toward me. But there's no figure; there's not even a trick of the light, because the light is clear and pale, too young and unaccustomed to its powers to tell any lies. The road is empty except for a few random campers, wandering toward the bathroom, toward the registration office, toward the lake. Such a strange thing to find in a desert.

# Operculum

# I

Every day I wait for your letter and it doesn't come. I hear the mail hitting the floor by the door at ten in the morning, or sometimes eleven. I always stay in bed until I hear the mail hit the floor. As I swing my feet out, as I'm going down the stairs, I'm thinking about picking up the envelope, about your name written in the top left corner in green ink, in spiky left-handed letters. The words I remember best in that green hand are: *Leah, I read the words you wrote in my journal like twenty times, and every time I was feeling better.* That's how I knew it was you who wrote obscenities on the door to the activity monitors' office, even though you said over and over that you didn't do it. That's how I knew it was you who wrote *I love Leah 4 ever* on all the corkboards in the c building; morning after morning for five summer weeks I let you out of class and I saw you swipe the chalk for that purpose.

If that letter ever comes, I'll carry it up the stairs and back into bed, and I'll tell Edmund, *I got a letter from Olivier.* I'll open it slowly; maybe I'll even read some to Edmund, to show him. Maybe I'll read it like twenty times, every time feeling better.

What really happens is, I come back up the cold stairs with a magazine or a gas bill and I get in the bed and make you promises: Olivier, listen to me, okay, listen. I won't know the difference. You can tell me all kinds of lies, and I'll believe you most of the time. You can make a fool out of me. I don't care about that. Even if everything you ever let me see was a lie, I won't lie to you.

Every time I hear a skateboard outside my living room window, I wait for your knock on my door. It's not impossible; you live in this city somewhere. I wonder if I should write to you first, ask if you're okay.

*Dear Olivier, I've been waiting for you but you don't come.*

*Dear Olivier, I hope that since you met me your life has become happy, even though I'm not there.*

*Dear Olivier, I miss you.*

There was a time I wrote things to you, in the journal I made you hand in every Friday for five weeks. Every Friday afternoon, I returned to my and Edmund's little hardwood apartment, our temporary Ottawa apartment that smelled of croissants from the bakery downstairs. I opened a beer and took it, with nineteen journals and my cigarettes, and the green lighter you gave me in class one day, out to the blue wire bench on the balcony, overlooking a wide parking lot that you could easily have come to with your skateboard if you'd wanted. I miss that Ottawa balcony. Here in Montreal I have nothing but a gravel rooftop and a blue plastic couch.

I always read your journal first. I believed everything you wrote. I wrote you things that were always true, things I thought you might want to hear.

*Have you ever picked one of those big pale seashells up off the beach? You can't see through them, but if you hold them up to the sun, light passes through. I sometimes think you're held together by one of those shells. The only thing it lets out is the light coming from inside you. It's blinding. If you don't open, it's going to burn you alive.*

I sometimes wish I'd taken that journal to the print shop and copied every page to keep with me forever, but I wrote it for you; it was a gift. I remember almost everything I wrote. The things you wrote, though, didn't always hang together so well, and they're not as clear for me now.

I sometimes wish I'd known how to stop writing and talk to you on the steps outside the c building, under the crabapple tree in front of the cafeteria, at your desk when you and I were the only ones in the room. Your face always snapped itself shut. Almost always. The times when it didn't, I understood that I wasn't a fool.

Every morning I leave the house for some reason, and I see you everywhere. I sit in a café and your face looks in through the window. You stand there watching me, and I watch you, and then I knock over my water glass and climb over the sill to embrace you. I carry my laundry home, a yellow sheet-sack the size of a hippo slung over my shoulder, and you come toward me, your skateboard diagonal across your thin chest, your little tawny wormbraids springing out all over your head, and you see me but you turn your gloomy face away and walk past. My whole body follows you. I spill my socks on the ground and call, *Olivier?* Your head turns halfway around; you're trying not to recognize me. I say, *Don't you have a kiss for your teacher?* You almost smile, but you don't come back. You keep going.

i

I'm walking down Ste-Catherine. I haven't thought of you all day. It's a month from now, maybe two. I'm trying to light a cigarette out of one corner of my mouth, but I can't stop moving because

I'm on my way . . . where? Somewhere important, something I can't miss, something that means everything because you've gone, you've escaped. I can't even recall your voice so rough in your adolescent chest, or your lead-gold hair. But I'm not thinking of that. I'm watching the crazies on the corner of St-Laurent . . . every time I pass here I pull my coat tighter, and it's just become the time for coats. I haven't thought of you for weeks, or if I have, it's only been once in a while. You've never written; occasionally I pick up a pen and put it down. But I'm not thinking of that. It's chill and grey, the sky's getting lower and lower, and I'm thinking of point B, at the end of this line.

The kids sitting on the concrete blocks ask for change, for a cigarette. The pack's in my hand. Do I stop? I'm still moving. I usually give something, because when I see someone drop a dollar into a mittened hand I think, *That must be a nice person.* But I'm busy. What could be so important? I've never cared about the next bus, or being on time for the suit at Hydro-Quebec who thinks the conditional form will change his life. But I must be different now; something matters.

The kids in cracked leather and Docs are polite. I stop, finally, and flip the pack open. Sorry, don't have time to pull out my green lighter. The one you gave me. There you are.

*Olivier?*

Your head snaps up. That's a look I know, the I-didn't-do-it-I-swear look. *W-what?*

I'm stone. I'm a plant afraid to open. *Olivier?*

I can't tell if you don't know me or if you don't want to. This is what I was afraid of, what I've forgotten I'm afraid of. You looking at me: *Do I have room for her?* You've always been so golden, so fed, but you look like you've been sleeping on something hard, when you've been sleeping. That scab is still on your forearm, that scab you used to pick at in class until it bled, the scab that was there the whole five weeks I knew you. Where's your skateboard?

*It's me,* I say. Your face has gone crazy. *Leah.* Stop that. Stop trying to know what I want you to say. I wait a whole minute, watching you half-open, then half-close. *What are you doing here?*

You look at the ground, shrug, smile that scared smile, the I-guess-the-best-thing-to-do-is-laugh smile. The other kids are watching, curious or contemptuous.

*I'm hanging around here for a while,* you say.

I take a breath, crouch down on my heels, take a breath again. *I don't mean to … I just . . . I've been thinking about you.* I almost correct myself; I do that, when I lie, even when it's best to just leave it alone. *I've been meaning to write to you.*

You glance up with raised eyebrows. Are you really surprised? There's no way to know when you're making things up. Then I remember the promise I made to you silently, in the night, when you weren't there: I will believe you. I won't know the difference.

Am I embarrassing you, here on this concrete corner? I wanted to write you a letter because I wanted you to know that it wasn't over, but maybe it was over for you. Now it's not over any more. That's why I imagine these things.

I say, *Where's your skateboard?*

You laugh, and look up again. This is the smile I waited for all day, every day, the smile that opens the door a crack. *I sold it,* you say.

*You sold it?*

*I needed stuff.*

You wrote to me once in your journal about your cousin who used to be a junkie. You wrote to me that you knew better than that. Did you only know better when you were telling me?

*Did you run away?*

You shrug. *I'm not gonna stay here forever.*

What do you know about forever, I think. You who told me you'd probably quit school, go to Vancouver, be a professional

141

skateboarder. *Are you going to stay here tonight?*

*There's a place I go. With these girls.* You gesture to the girls on either side of you, the blonde with the black roots and the stud in her lip, the stubble-headed girl knocking the heels of her Docs against the block. They both dart their eyes at me and move off, talking in French, in low, rough voices, glancing back. You look from one side to the other, then down between your knees again.

*Does your mother know where you are?* You give a little sigh. What do you think I'm doing? What am I doing? *I'm sorry; I'm just so surprised. I never imagined . . .* and I stop before I tell more lies.

*I'm okay. I've got friends out here; we take care of each other.*

I have a choice. I can say, I'll come back and see you tomorrow, wait for me here. Or I can say something else.

ᡸ

We get in the door and you look around like this is the scariest place you've ever been. What are you wearing? A dirty T-shirt and those nylon sports pants with the stripes, with the zippers at the ankles. Maybe some thick-soled expensive sneakers, maybe that cozy yellow sweatshirt that I couldn't believe you wore to class in the thirty-five degrees of July; you snapped at me once when I asked if you were hot. Take your hair out of those braids. When it all flies up it glows like a mineral the world wants desperately to find.

This is a bad idea, a good idea, a bad idea. Should I offer you tea, water, beer? I don't keep soft drinks in the house. I doubt I have anything you'd want to eat.

*We should call your mother,* I say.

You look around you, your face closed.

I offer you a shower, and you nod. I offer you food. *We*

*eat vegetarian here,* I tell you. You make a face and I laugh. *I can make you a sandwich. Peanut butter, cheese . . . what have you been eating?*

> *When we get some money we go to McDo.*

Christ.

*Peanut butter would be good.*

I bring you a purple towel. Clearly you have no clean clothes. Edmund is about four inches taller than you, but more or less the same size around. I lay his clothes out on the bed: a T-shirt, a pair of paint-stained track pants, cotton socks. All white and grey, nothing you could laugh at. I go to the kitchen and take down the bread, stand there facing the bricks for a while, listening to the water hit the shower wall. I'm trembling. For as far back as I remember, joy has always made me panic. What will Edmund say when he comes home? What if you steal my computer, his computer, the CDs from my bookcase? Your mother's phone number must be in the phone book, but how do I know she's what's required? There's the law, but right now the law can kiss my ass. What if you start spinning out on my couch? Or foaming at the mouth like something out of *The Basketball Diaries*? What if I'm a fool? What if I wake up tomorrow morning and you're still here and I don't love you any more?

I put together a peanut butter sandwich; it's all natural and I picture you spitting it out. I cut an apple into quarters and wonder if you'll resent me for treating you like an eight-year-old. I hiss open a microbrewed beer and pour it into two glasses. I don't look as the bathroom door opens and you slip into the bedroom. I put your lunch on the table and take out a cigarette. I have to think I have to think. Any moment now I'll hear the key in the lock and the shudder of the door and I'll have to explain *It's November, It's cold, He's just a child, You know what he means to me.*

When I was six, my mother decided to start taking in foster children, and my father didn't speak to anyone for seven years, until all the children were gone.

Have I ever told you that my brother's name is Oliver and I didn't love him nearly enough?

Here you come. I flutter around. I place the glass of beer in front of you and say, briskly, *Don't tell anyone.* I start to wash a plate.

Whenever you were the first to come back to class, I ruffled through papers, back and forth, walked out with nowhere to go, couldn't find the chalk, or on a good day I came to your desk and sat on my heels just like I did in front of that concrete block today, folded my arms under my chin and said something void: *Where's your essay? Did you bring a pack of cards like I asked you? What time is your mother coming to pick you up?*

You bite your sandwich behind me and don't mention that it doesn't taste like what you thought you were asking for. *Do you live here alone?* you ask. I know this is not a question about me so much as it is a question about you, about what's going to happen to you next.

I shake my head, but my back's to you as I rinse cutlery. *No. You remember Edmund.* I glance over my shoulder and you frown. *The teacher, the tall skinny guy. You remember that day when our class was outside, and you and I were drawing that Trivial Pursuit board on the asphalt in the courtyard? And he hung out the window to talk to me and you told me to stop flirting.*

You choke and swallow. *He's your boyfriend?*

*Yep.*

*Shit. Did you meet him there?*

I laugh. *That would have been speedy.*

*What?*

Sometimes I forget this isn't your language. *I've known him for years.*

You're not touching your beer. I sit down at the table and take a sip of mine. My cigarette's smouldering in a saucer. I put it out.

# Operculum

*What's he gonna say when he sees me?*

I shrug. *He's pretty easygoing.*

*What?*

*He's a relaxed kind of guy. He'll remember you; I talked to him about you sometimes.* I talked about nothing but you for five weeks; that's more likely than anything to be the problem.

*You did?* You go a little pink. Your smile almost surfaces in your eyes. Grey? Almost silver, almost slate, sunk back behind gold lashes like a bear in a cave. *What did you say about me?*

I take another sip, try not to blush, can't help it. *I said that you were so smart and so difficult and so good at speaking English and that I hoped to god someday you'd figure out what to do with yourself.*

You're red. Your sandwich is almost finished. *I guess now you think I'm a big loser.*

*I can't imagine anything you could do that would make me think you were a loser.*

I've always said that love is something you create, something you make together. You and I, we've made nothing together. This is all me. Even this conversation, the only time you've said anything to me with your mouth, is something I'm saying to myself with my mind.

You snort, and pick up a piece of apple, then put it down. *I left school. My mother kicked me out. I don't have any friends. I don't even have my skateboard any more.*

*Why'd you leave school?*

You shrug. *Because I hated it.*

*I know that. Why'd you hate it?*

You look out the window at the flat rooftop, grey with gravel, cold-looking. The neighbour on a balcony across the alley hanging her sheets out. *It was different with you.*

*You didn't like the schoolish part with me much, either.*

*Yeah, well. I'm not good at studying. I'd rather be having fun.*

*Most of us would.*

*No. You're a teacher. If you didn't like school, why would you be a teacher?*

Once in class when we were doing drills of the conditional, you were asleep on your arms. I said, *Olivier. You weren't listening, so you didn't understand. Conditional.* You peered up, bleary, and said, *But if you had been listening, you would have understood.* Then you went back to sleep. The rest of the class were silent, agog. Me too.

*Why was it different with me?* I ask.

*You were always smiling. Even when I was being a shit.*

*You weren't a shit. Maybe you were a shit to some people, but you were never a shit in my class.*

*I didn't do my homework.*

*What do I care if you do your homework?*

*Teachers care.*

*Hmm. Olivier?*

*Yeah?*

*What are you going to do now?*

*I don't know.* You look out the window again.

*Your mother needs to know where you are.*

*She kicked me out.*

*Why?*

*We had a fight.*

*Do you mind if I ask what the fight was about?* This is my classroom trick; maybe you remember it: waiting until the answer comes, no matter how long it takes.

*She's still seeing my dad.*

*Ah.*

*She wants me and him to be friends.*

*I would have expected her to be over that.*

*What?*

*I'm surprised she doesn't understand why that would be hard for you.*

*Yeah, well.*

I take another cigarette and offer one to you; you accept. The green lighter you gave me is on the table. I hold it up. *Do you remember this?* You look, blankly, then look some more, smile, nod a little. You take it from my hand and light my cigarette.

Then I ask, *Do you ever see Jérôme any more?*

You shake your head.

*You two were such good friends.*

*Not really.*

*What do you mean?*

*Forget it.*

I wait a moment. Your golden face is tightening around the eyes.

*It's because,* you say, *you know? It's easy to be friends with girls. Boys are . . . forget it. Never mind.* We puff in silence. *Leah?*

*Yeah?*

*I'm really tired.*

It's true. Your eyes aren't tightening; they're closing.

Edmund's on his way home. I, at thirty, am getting old. You're going to sleep in our bed; today and tonight there will not be enough room in this house. But then, there's not enough room in the world.

You're sitting beside me on the blue plastic couch on the gravel rooftop and I take your face in my hands although I know you'd never let me do that.

You come to sit on the foot of my bed and tell me that you want something from me. What do I say?

The key turns in the lock. I put out my cigarette. How do I see his face as it comes through the hall to the kitchen? He puts his hand on the knob of the bedroom door, then looks up, puzzled, at the door's closed surface. *There's someone in there,* I say.

When you're trying to decide what needs to be expressed so you can stay out of trouble, confusion bursts from your face like a Christmas cracker. When he's trying to decide what needs to be repressed so he can cause the least trouble for others, his mouth becomes stiff and cage-like, and his limbs become conscious of themselves. Do I let him wonder for a moment? Could he wonder anything that could compare with you?

*Do you remember Olivier?*

Now, it's possible to imagine him replying, *Your brother?* That would be convenient, and would be a nice opportunity for me to say some things I want to say, about you and about my brother. But my brother's name is Oliver and I would never call him Olivier, so it's unlikely Edmund would make such a mistake. It's more likely he'd say: *Olivier from the summer?*

As I explain, are you awake and listening? I wouldn't check on you because that would be too creepy, teacher peering in on student as he sleeps, admiring the shapes of him under and over the blanket. If you're awake you can hear everything we say. What do you want us to say? It's better if you're asleep.

Edmund does something – takes out the Brita and pours a glass of water, eats an olive, opens the paper – and says, *I see.*

*How could I leave him there?*

*Well, you left all the other homeless kids in the world where they are.*

*You know what he means to me.*

*I know what he meant to you, but that was a defined space, a finite period. This is your life. And my life, I might add.* He stops eating or drinking or rustling and leans against the wall. *What are you going to do?*

*I don't know.*

*Do you trust him?*

*I don't know. He could be on heroin for all I know, or working for a burglary ring. I'm not asking you to take it on. I'm just asking you to let me do this for a bit.*

Edmund nods, his mouth growing stiffer. *Well, maybe I should go.* He slides into a chair, looks at me steadily for a while, and smiles. Just barely, as though he thinks he means it but is not sure. *This is yours,* he says. *You want him to yourself.*

⮧

When he's gone, you wake up and drift out with your braids in the air and pillowcase marks on your soft cheek. I'm making spaghetti for dinner. I ask you if you can cook. You shake your head. *I make eggs for breakfast sometimes,* you say. So I tell you that breakfast tomorrow is your job, and you nod and smile routinely.

Maybe I should feel obliged to entertain you, but certain things need to be addressed first. I ask how long you've been on the street, and you say you left home a couple of weeks ago, but stayed with a friend for a while, until her mother got tired of you and asked you to leave. You've been sleeping in a shelter since then, some place downtown those two girls took you to.

*And you've been begging?*

*What?*

*You've been asking for money on the streets, for food?*

*Mostly they shared with me. Girls get more than boys.*

*What do you mean?*

*People feel sorry for girls. Nobody ever gave me a cent. Louise says it's because of my clothes, because I look like a rich brat, but I think it's because people feel sorry for girls.*

*Hmm. And are you ever planning to go home?*

*I don't know.*

*Well, if you don't, what will you do?*

*I don't know.*

*Olivier. Street life is not pretty.*
*How would you know?*
Point for you. Good idiomatic structure, too.

I ask you what the other kids do, besides begging, and you say that some of them squeegee, that maybe you'll do that too. *And there are guys who come around asking for sex, but they think they can get it for cheap.*

*Do you feel okay about doing that?*
You don't look at me. *No.*
*No, really, Olivier.*
You look me in the eye. I've seen this before, the she'll-believe-me-if-I-look-her-in-the-eye tactic. *No. It's disgusting.*
Maybe you sound sincere because you believe yourself.

卍

I'll skip to bedtime because I don't know what to do with the hours in between. Watch TV? Talk about your future? Your future doesn't interest you. Should I take you around and introduce you to my friends? Your silence would engulf us all so completely that I'd have to take you home again. Call your mother? *Olivier, tomorrow we have to call your mother.*

This is your trap door. You nod, knowing already that it doesn't matter. We pull the futon into the living room. I help you with the sheets and blankets on, and we say goodnight.

Normally I sleep in the nude. Tonight this would not be appropriate. There are two possibilities: the blue flannel pyjamas or the white lace negligee. I hesitate. The pyjamas. After a moment, though, I undo the top two buttons of the shirt, because this is what I imagine, and I can prepare for the things I intend to happen.

I already know that I'll wake up in a few hours and you'll be in the doorway, in Edmund's white T-shirt and your own blue-checked boxer shorts that I've seen so many times above the waistband of your low-slung pants. You're backlit from the streetlights filtering and colliding through the hall, your star-brown hair out of its braids and standing on end. You're faceless in the dark. Limbs all thin shadows. *Leah?*

I roll over, rub my eyes as if surprised. *Olivier?*

This is the part I have a difficult time with, but it has to happen, otherwise the story is a waste and there's no reason for me to ever see you again. You have to find your way to the foot of the bed, and sit. You have to sit there for a few moments, searching, or waiting, or something. The question is, do you ask me? Or do I just pull the blankets back and say, *Come here?*

You lie down, your back to me, near enough for me to touch, far enough for me not to. I move in close, put an arm around the golden bones of your torso, put a cheek against your hair, and say, *Go to sleep, sweetheart.*

If I've understood everything correctly, that's what you do. I don't sleep, of course. I lie awake as long as I'm able. I'm imagining this, so I know this is the shortest and most precious thing I'll ever have. I'd be a fool to sleep through it.

⮨

Even if I'm sleeping, you'd never be able to move without my knowing, so perhaps I let you go. In the morning my computer's gone, because mine is portable and Edmund's is not. There's no note. You don't even leave Edmund's clothes.

If this were true, there would be things to do. Should I call your mother? Maybe I could look through my papers to find your address and discover I don't have it, and then I could be at a loss to remember your mother's name. And Edmund – there'd be a whole story about that. Ultimately, I'd have to decide whether I meant it when I said you could make a fool out of me.

This story, though, is a bit like those five real weeks when I had you. When it's over it's over, and what comes next has nothing to do with it.

There's one thing missing, one thing I've tried and tried to stick in. It doesn't fit anywhere. I need you to cry, to weep with realization or just exhaustion. I need to see that. But I can't manage it. Not in this one, anyhow.

## II

I wake up and watch the ceiling while Edmund sleeps. I wait for the sound of the mail. The last time I saw you was in Ottawa, seven days ago. You introduced me to your mother and I told her, *He's a brilliant boy.* I wanted to say all kinds of other things. She and I smoked cigarettes outside the cafeteria door and talked about the Quebec education system, your home together in Longueuil, and summers in Victoria. She looked like a movie star would have looked about ten years ago, with her crimped golden hair and French-manicured nails. I saw you ask her, afterwards, what we had been talking about, and I wished I'd given her something better to tell you.

You went to pack your bags while I said goodbye to eighteen students one by one. I went back to the parking lot and smoked and refused to go away with my friends until you came back and I could kiss you. I said *Take care of yourself* and you smiled and I thought I might try to pick you up and carry you away and you said *You too* and that was all and I went to a bar to drink beer with my boyfriend and hope I wouldn't miss you for the rest of my life. Or that I would.

Edmund is still asleep. There is no sound of letters falling.

I wonder if you let your mother read the things I wrote to you. I wonder if she ripped up your journal in a rage, or if someday I'll get a letter from her thanking me for saving you.

I have a brother named Oliver, and the last time I saw him he was sixteen years old, and a lot like you.

# Operculum

## ii

It's September, school's starting, and I'm just hanging and waiting. It's almost fall, but it's still too hot. I'm in my grey chair that rolls away because the floor won't stand up straight. Today I'm filling time: shuffling course outlines, ripping up paper for bookmarks and sticking them between the pages of brand new grammar activity books at strategic points: games for the perfect tenses; articles; first conditional. I think about a walk, about a book in a café, but it's one of those afternoons when I wouldn't really be escaping from anything so why bother. The phone rings.

*Is this Madame Leah Dalton?*

*Yes, it is.*

*Madame Dalton, my name is Justine Quesnel.*

Have I forgotten you? When she says *Justine Quesnel*, do I know who Justine Quesnel is? Do I wait for her to explain:

*I met you this summer in Ottawa. You were the teacher of my son, Olivier.*

Or do I say immediately:

*Oh, Madame Quesnel, hello. How are you?*

To which she would reply:

*Do you remember me? I met you this summer in Ottawa. You were the teacher of my son, Olivier.*

*Of course I remember you.*

We exchange pleasantries, and I ask after Olivier.

*Olivier is . . . is fine, I think. He remembers you well; he speaks of you much.*

*Really. That's very flattering.* I'm trying to imagine him speaking much about anything, much less me.

*That is why I am calling you. Olivier and I have been speaking . . . he needs help with school. As you know, he is not always very . . . motivated. I told you, I think, that he goes to English high school this year.*

*Yes. I think it's an excellent idea.*

*Yes, I think so. But I am thinking that he will maybe need some extra help. I want him to have a private . . . tutor? Do we use this word? He doesn't want to do extra work, of course, but for me it is very important. I think this is the best way. When I talked to him, he said he would like it if it is somebody like you. So I found your number in the* bottin. *I hope it is not a mistake, to call you at home. I don't know if you have some time, or how much you ask for your lessons.*

*Madame Quesnel . . . I'm not sure what you are asking. Olivier already speaks English very well.*

*If you could just consult with him, just a couple of hours a week, and help him. His sister went to English high school and her first year was very hard. This year is his finishing . . . of course, if you don't have time, I understand. Maybe you could recommend me someone else.*

ᚱ

Where do I meet you, and what do we say to each other? I don't want you to prove me wrong, to make me wonder why you ever wrote *I love Leah 4 ever* in chalk on any surface of the world. Whatever you wanted from me (and you did want something, I saw it that day under the crabapple tree when I sat on the ground and you stood there, plucking at the apples above me, not wanting to go away), it had nothing to do with English or any other language.

Let's put it here: I come to your house. Your mother pays my cab fare from Longueuil metro. The house will have to be big and ostentatious like the Mercedes your mother came in to take you away from me. People in this town don't have servants or chandeliers, but there would be a home entertainment system the size of a forest, a million easy ways to leave your life. Expensive carpets of dubious taste. A kitchen no one cooks in, a freezer full of microwavable food, boxes from St-Hubert Chicken left on the counter from lunch. Your room I probably won't get to see.

We'll set up in the basement recreation room between the forty-inch television and the cocktail-style bar with the shiny black top and coaster-holes. Your mother will click her long nails – conch-rose, today – against the conspicuously cheap, dishwasher-spotted glass in which she brings me water. The table is meant for playing Euchre or Monopoly, but the chairs are dark wood with cushioned seats, cushions embroidered with big sunset orange and brown and pink flowers, like a tired dining room set not worn enough to throw out. Your mother will disappear up the shallow stairs that turn at the top. You'll pile your books in a closed stack, open and shut a notebook or two, try to flip your pen in circles with your fingertips and watch it fly under the table, dig under and not come up.

*Hi,* I'll say.

*Hi.* You'll stay under the table for a little longer. When you surface your face will be red, your eyes on your pen as you try to twirl it again.

Oral exams were like this. No matter what present you'd given me or joke you'd made only minutes before, the moment we sat alone together you only needed to avoid saying the wrong thing, which meant you had to avoid saying anything at all.

*How are you doing?*

*Fine.* You stop twirling your pen and stare at the tabletop.

*How's school going?*

*Okay.*

*Which school are you at?*

You name some school. That scab is still on your forearm, long and ugly; you're picking at it with your fingertips and your eyes, and it bleeds.

*What are you studying?*

You snort. *The usual stuff.*

*For example?*

You put on your this-is-very-tiresome-for-me voice. *English math social studies moral education physical education science French. . . .*

*They're making you take French?*

*I'm in the advanced class.*

*What do you do in French?*

*Nothing. It's boring.*

*I guess so. What about English?*

*It's fine, I guess. I don't know. It's only been a week.*

*Are you doing literature? Composition? Grammar? Research papers?*

*It's called prose. We write sentences.*

*Sentences.*

*Yeah. Topic sentences. Next we're doing paragraphs. He says we'll do essays and short stories later.*

*Oh, I see. Well, you like to write, don't you?*

*Yeah. I guess.*

*Can I see what you've been doing?*

You pull out a notebook: wrong one; another: wrong one; another. *I guess I must have left it in my locker.*

What am I doing here? *Olivier, what am I doing here?*

*What?* You look up with the I-didn't-do-it look – lips a bit open, grey eyes wide.

*I know what your mother wants me to do, but from the looks of it, I'm not sure what we're going to accomplish.* This is not your smile blush, it's your oh-shit-what-do-I-do-now blush. *I'm really happy your mother called. I'd be honoured to help you with your work. But I'm not sure what you need me for. What do you need me for?*

I wait.

*I guess for the stuff I don't understand.*

*Okay. But you have teachers; you can ask them questions.*

*Yeah. Well. I don't like my teachers much.*

*What do you mean?*

*I don't know.*

*No,* really, *Olivier.*

*I don't know. They're just teachers. Sometimes they go too fast. And anyway, this stuff is so boring.*

I nod. Yes. Yes, I imagine sometimes it is. Were you really thinking about quitting school this year?

*Yeah.*

*Why didn't you?*

You shrug. *I don't know. I didn't really know what else to do.*

*You said you were thinking of going to B.C.*

*Yeah.*

*What for?*

*To skateboard. I have some friends out there.*

*So why didn't you?*

*I don't know.*

*Come* on.

*I don't* know. *It would have been too hard. I don't have any money. What do you want me to say?*

*Aha. That's just the problem. I don't want you to say anything in particular. I want to know what's going on. It's not easy to talk to you, you know.*

There it is. Your smile sneaks up on you and you're coming out, you're knocking at the back of your burnt-star eyes. *I know,* you say.

*Help me out here. Your mother isn't going to pay me to sit here and watch you move your notebooks back and forth. Tell me something you need to do, and we'll do it.*

I wonder if you're going to dissolve, but I hang on to it. Don't go yet.

*Well, there's my history homework.*

*Bingo. Hand it over.*

⤳

One day it's warm and we sit on the deck outside, next to the pool which has already been covered over with a big night-blue tarpaulin. *Do you like to swim?* I ask.

*Not really. My sister and my mom use it.*

*Hmm.* I tap my fingers against the table top for a while. *I'd love to have a pool. We had one when I was young. But . . . have I ever told you that my brother's name is Oliver?*

I think I got your attention.

*When he was about four he almost drowned in the pool. I jumped in after him, but of course you don't do that with someone who's drowning. If my father hadn't finally noticed, I suppose we'd both be dead now. Dad got some guys to come and fill the pool in just a couple of days later. We thought he was punishing us.*

Your grey eyes are wide. *How old were you?*

I don't think you've ever asked a question about me before.

*I would have been six. It was the same year the foster kids started to arrive.*

ᘰ

Your mother keeps going up and down the stairs and one day, for no reason I can invent right now, I say to you, *You and your mother are very close, aren't you?*

You look up as though I pinched you. Then you flush like a sunrise. *Well, yeah, I guess. She's cool.*

*She's so glamorous-looking. She seems very young.*

*Well, she had me when she was fifteen.*

That would make her. . . .

I won't consider that right now

*She's like my friend,* you say, *more than my mom.*

*But she's very concerned about you, like a mom is.*

*Yeah, well, sometimes I think she's more concerned about looking like a good mom. Sometimes I think if it was just me and her in the world, she'd let me do whatever the fuck I want.*

So I'm here because your mom wants to look like a good mom?

You grin. *No.* Then you look down at the table top, flushing.

*So why am I here?*

*Because she thinks you're good for me.* You trace the table edge nearest you with your fingertip, back and forth.

*Why?* I ask.

You glance up under the lead-blond of your eyebrows. You bite your lip. Your voice is barely audible. *After I came back from Ottawa she said I looked so happy.*

We look at each other for a while, both of us turning all shades of red. Then you look down at the table again.

I say, *Ottawa was kind of a dream world, wasn't it?*

*Yeah.*

*I was afraid that when you went home you'd go back to being all tied up inside yourself. And you did, sort of, didn't you?*

*Sort of. But you know what?*

*What?*

*When I feel like shit, I take out my journal and read all the things you wrote to me. Sometimes I read them like twenty times. And every time I'm feeling better.*

Afterwards I go home to where Edmund is making dinner and he smiles at me patiently. He asks about you sometimes, and sometimes I tell him the things you said to me. I feel a need, on occasion, to prove to him that I'm not inventing you. Sometimes he seems to be waiting, behind his face, for me to come to my senses.

One day in the middle of your descriptive essay you tell me that the journal is gone.

The first thing I think is that she's the storm that keeps you in one spot crouching with your arms over your head, just as we always think it's mothers who control the world and fuck everything up. Forget that your father beat the crap out of you. It's your mother with her hair like a swaying field of peaches'n'cream corn who is keeping you panicked and useless.

That night in Ottawa when we stood outside the cafeteria doors as the banquet went on inside, she mentioned that her husband did something or other. I hadn't been aware that she had a husband. You'd never mentioned a stepfather, but you'd never answered the question I wrote in your journal, about where your father was living, either. I never see any man around here but you, if you qualify.

*Olivier, didn't your mother tell me that she's married?*

You look surprised. *Yeah. She's married to my dad.*

*She's still married to your dad.*

*Yeah.*

*But he doesn't live here any more.*

*No, not now.*

*What do you mean, not now?*

*Well, Mom . . . he was, well, you know. He used to hit her a lot.*

*And you too.*

*Yeah, me too.*

He left a couple of years ago, you tell me. They're not divorced, but you don't see him.

*Never?*

*Hardly ever.*

*What do you mean, hardly ever?*

*He came by a couple of months ago, just before I left for Ottawa. He was pretty nice that day. Sometimes he can be pretty okay.*

*Olivier, he beat you.*

*Yeah, well, he's not touching me any more.*

*Does your mother still love him? Sorry. Shit, I'm sorry, this is really none of my business.*

You're looking at your pen spinning around in your fingertips. You're getting pretty good at that. *It's okay. I don't know. I guess so. He's her husband, you know? She says that when you love someone you love them. You don't just stop.*

*Yeah. I know. Olivier?*

*Yeah?*

*I remember almost everything I wrote to you in that journal. If you want me to, I'll write it all down for you again.*

You smile. I want to clench you until I crack something that's holding you together. *It's okay,* you say. *I remember almost everything too.*

ೞ

Now you'd think that I'd be able to choose to stay there with you forever. But that's not what happens. Maybe that's not what I choose. Instead your mother calls to say you won't be needing my services any more.

*He is doing well in school now.*

*He's not doing nearly as well as he could. Of course, maybe I'm not doing the job you hoped. But he seems so much happier lately, and I'm enjoying my time with him. Is there something else on your mind?*

*Well, in truth, I don't feel that you and Olivier communicate in a way that is exactly . . . acceptable.*

*What do you mean? I'm very sorry if I've overstepped any boundaries.*

*Pardon me? I don't understand.*

*I'm sorry. I mean I'm very sorry if I've done anything I shouldn't have.*

Silence. Then she sighs.

*You ask Olivier very intimate questions about our family relationships. And recently I read . . . he showed me the things that you wrote to him this summer, during his course. I found them . . . strange.*

What things, exactly?

*I think you understand what I am saying.*

Telling him that he's a good person, that he should be proud of himself, that I'm proud of him?

*You cannot be proud of someone you know for only such a short time. That is the privilege of parents and friends.*

That's very well-put, I think. *Justine, I care about your son very much, but it has nothing to do with the things you're suggesting.*

Please don't come any more.

Can I believe that you'd come to my house now, maybe put your head in my lap and say that you miss me? Maybe. Would you come and tell me that your mother was afraid? Unlikely. I want you to cry, to put your arms around me and weep. But you wouldn't do that, for any reason.

One thing I can imagine, though, is that I would run into you on the street someday. Maybe years from now. How will you look when you're twenty years old? Will you still have a skateboard under your arm? All right, I see you a year from now in Sport Experts, where I go to buy new cross-trainers. There you are checking out snowboards and what am I doing in the snowboard section? Looking for you. You know me before I say your name this time. And there's that smile I spend all my time waiting for, and you open the doors of your starburst silver eyes and come all the way out. I walk over to you and you walk over to me and maybe you hug me . . . I don't even remember what it feels like to hug you. You put your face against my neck and I feel all the silk of your hair. I say, *Olivier, are you okay?*

And you say, *Yeah, I'm okay. I'm sorry about my mom.*

*I didn't understand that. Did she think . . . what did she think? What did you think? Olivier, if I ever did anything that made you . . . did you think I . . . listen. You know that it had nothing to do with any of that. I don't want you to ever think that anything I said to you was about sex. I don't care about you because I want to have sex with you.*

I made a promise to you once, but you weren't there and you didn't hear. Besides, I don't know what's true.

You say, *It's okay if you want to have sex with me. I'm not a baby.*

And now I really want to rip the whole world apart and put it back together into something different. *That's not the point,* I say. I put out one hand and hope you let me put my palm against the warmth of that peachhoney skin of your cheek. I have a choice.

This is what I'd say:

*If I were sixteen years old, you would be the answer to all my dreams. In five years, let's have this conversation again. Learn to tell the truth. Then we'll talk.*

This is what I'd say:

*I don't want you to be responsible for me. I want you to take care of yourself.*

But most likely, I'd say this, I'd say:

*Do you still see Jérôme?*

Which would you rather hear?

It doesn't matter; in five years' time you won't remember my name. Even now there's nothing I can give you, nothing I could be that you need anymore. Nothing for me to be strong for. We could stand there in Sports Experts for hours, or I could take you for a coffee, or I could write you letters that your mother will read and then put down the garbage disposal. Whatever I choose, it changes nothing. My time is already up.

## III

It's been eleven days since the last time I saw you in Ottawa, and today I only thought of you briefly this morning. I woke up after the mail and when I looked, there was nothing. Then I forgot you until now. It's late, and Edmund is peering through the kitchen window, wondering why I'm out here on the blue plastic couch on the rooftop, smoking all alone, as far as he can see. And when I imagine you standing in my doorway, all I feel is vagueness.

Sometimes I wonder if I'm a fool, and then I remember:

We all went out in the courtyard to play Trivial Pursuit and you helped me draw the board on the asphalt. Then when we sat down on the grass, you pushed into the circle to sit next to me, and brushed the yellow grass from the leg of my jeans. Edmund leaned out the window to talk to me at that very moment; if I ever doubt that you were there I'll ask him, and I expect him to tell me that it's true. Even Edmund couldn't deny it, and I don't see how he could forget.

You gave me your green lighter as a present and when Jérôme said, *Stop flirting,* you laughed.

I was sitting under that crabapple tree correcting papers and you sneaked up behind the tree and put your hand on me to scare me and you did. Jérôme pushed you and you hit your head. I said it served you right. I should have laughed, but I couldn't because my heart was going to pop out of my mouth.

Jérôme came to borrow my lighter, the green lighter you gave me, and you were the one who brought it back to me. Did I smile with surprise? I hope I did. You hung there plucking at the crabapples on the tree while I asked you about your exam, asked you about your paper, and you answered my questions as though you wanted to be there talking to me. Why didn't I say something else? Why didn't I ask if it was okay for me to write to you in your journal as though I knew you? Why didn't I ask you again if you were okay?

You never wrote obscenities on my door. All you wrote was *I love Leah 4 ever* in big white chalk.

And you wrote, *Leah, I read it like twenty times. . . .*

And when we were leaving each other we didn't know what to say. I didn't know what to say.


iii


I write you a letter.

*Dear Olivier,*

*Ottawa seems like a dream now, but I'm writing because I am thinking about you and wondering how you are doing. You wrote in your journal this summer that you are thinking of going to B.C. instead of going back to school. Did you make a decision about that? Your mother said you'd be going to English high school this year, which I think is a great idea. But I know that school isn't for everybody. Write me a letter sometime and let me know how you are.*

*Leah*

Then I can't decide. Sometimes a letter comes through the mail slot, but I think it works better this way: you and Jérôme come to see me. It's not inconceivable. When I gave you all my address on the last day of class, you made a joke about coming to visit, and with Jérôme, you might feel safe. You both shout *Leah!* when I open the door, and I shout *Boys! Come in!* I don't quite know what to do with you because I don't have any soft drinks in the house, but I bring you upstairs. Edmund decides to go have coffee somewhere, or maybe it's a warm day and he says hi and then sits at his computer and I take you out onto the roof to smoke cigarettes and watch the neighbour hang out her sheets. The two of you are laughing and nudging each other in a way that suits Jérôme but doesn't suit you, and although I'm glad you're not here alone because what would I say to you, I wish a little that you didn't need someone else. I offer you a drink and Jérôme the athlete says water, so you say water too. We sit with our water on the blue plastic couch on the rooftop and you and I smoke our cigarettes. I ask Jérôme about his hockey scholarship and his girlfriend and then I ask you what you're doing, and you tell me you're going to British Columbia.

I nod. *You're not going back to school?*

*No. You know I hate school.*

*Yes, I know. What are you going to do in B.C.?*

You're going to skateboard, you say, and you have friends there, in Victoria. *Victoria,* I say. *Really. My parents live in Victoria.*

*Oh yeah?*

*Well, in a suburb. Saanich. Where are you staying?*

*I don't know. I'll stay with my friend for a while. I'll need to find a job, I guess.*

*I guess.*

You're going in three weeks. You have a ticket already, bought with money you won in a skateboard competition.

*First prize,* Jérôme says. *You should see him, Leah.*

*I've heard,* I say.

A week later, I write you this letter:

*Dear Olivier,*

*I've been thinking about the conversation we had the other day. If you really want a job, I might have a suggestion for you. My parents take in boarders at their house in Saanich; that is, they rent rooms to people. The rent is cheap, but I talked to them yesterday and they'd like to make a deal with you. They need someone to*

*do jobs around the house – cleaning, gardening, cutting the grass,
doing repairs, etc. If you'd do that for them, they'd give you a room
and meals for free and also pay you a bit of pocket money. They
don't have any boarders now except my brother; you'd share the
bathroom with him. (Have I ever told you that my brother's name
is Oliver?)*

*I'll call you next week. If you're interested, I'll come out
to Victoria with you and introduce you to them. Think about it
carefully. They're excited about having you. And I know you think
you're nothing but trouble, but my parents aren't stupid. They've
pretty much seen it all.*

*Leah*

Now why would I do that? So my father could fashion himself a
new bubble? So my brother could see himself at sixteen all over
again and either have a nervous breakdown or teach you to be a
more skillful and conscienceless criminal than you already are?

I'd do it because I don't care that you might be bad for
people. Because I want, at any price, to send my life and your life
running off in the same direction.

We wouldn't take the plane together. You've already got your
ticket, and besides, what would we do for five hours side by
side, listening to Miramax movies through tinny headphones,
you making fun of my ugly vegetarian plane food? How would
we fall asleep without touching each other on the armrest? No.
We meet at the ferry terminal in Tsawwassen and you're dressed
so clean and beautiful, your red cap backwards on your head,
your skateboard hanging under one arm. You're smiling. I've
seen that smile before. It was one Monday morning, and the
activity monitors stopped me outside the class and asked me to
send you upstairs. I came to see you and Jérôme at your desks.

You handed me your green lighter and said, *Here. You said you lost yours.* And I said, *Why thank you.* And Jérôme said, *Olivier, stop flirting.* Your mouth half opened and your eyes were sly and everything that always shut me out of your face forgot to protect you. All that radiance that's eating you alive burst free. Then I sent you off to be punished.

*Hi.*

*Hi.*

You don't look sullen. You look shy. Happy. Brave.

Long ago, I wrote my brother Oliver a letter. He was sixteen, the same age you are now. I wrote him a letter saying that I was sorry I hadn't taken care of him. Saying that I had loved him, I did love him, and no matter what, I would think about him. And I wrote this: *You have to do what you have to do.*

That last time, I wrote in your journal: BE BRAVE.

We get on the ferry and we don't say much, but it doesn't matter. *Have you done this before?* I ask you. You nod. *Did you see killer whales?*

You snort. *No. Did you?*

*No, but I intend to see some today.*

You grin. *Okay. Let's see some today.*

Am I going too far here? I don't think so. I don't think I'm making it up; I think this might be you.

We go out on the sixth deck. You sit back on one of the emergency equipment crates, your skateboard across your lap. Where are your bags? You have a backpack that you put under your feet. I left my stuff in Vancouver because I don't intend to stay long; I just have a daypack with a clean shirt, some underwear, and a book. I lean out over the railing and watch the water gallop by. The sun is beating down and the breeze is warm; my parents told me on the phone that this is the most perfect summer they've seen in the five years they've been here.

The important thing is: *I'm* hardly afraid of *you* at all.

We don't see any killer whales, and we don't talk much.

There's a lot I want to say, and you don't have a journal for me to write in any more. Will I go sit beside you on the crate?

*Leah?*

I go sit beside you on the crate. *Yes.*

*Your parents must be really cool.*

I shrug. *They're cool in lots of ways. They're human beings, though. Can you look after yourself? I suppose it's a bit late to ask you this now.*

*I guess I can.*

*Olivier?*

*Yeah.*

*Did I tell you that you're a lot like my little brother?*

You blush, your eyes like coins. *You wrote that his name's Oliver.*

*You're going to be living with my brother and I don't know that you'll be good for each other.*

You frown. *What?* And you laugh.

*Do you remember when I wrote in your journal that you had a potential for happiness?*

*Yeah.*

*I think my brother's potential for happiness is almost used up.*

*What?*

*My brother was like you when he was sixteen. Since then, he hasn't really lived a happy life. When I look at you, I'm afraid you're going to run out of happiness. Do you understand?*

You laugh again. *No.*

I'm losing hold. Wait. Don't go. What can I say? Should I drop it? Is this the moment for the killer whales to appear? No. I need to find a way to say this.

*Okay. I don't want to give you a speech. Do you mind if I just talk to you about this?*

*Okay.*

*No,* really, *Olivier.*

*No, I don't mind.* And you don't. I can tell.

*Are you happy that you're going somewhere new?*
You're in the world, you're here with me, you're smiling.
*Sure.*
*Right. I'm happy about it too. Ever since I met you I've been caring what happens to you, and wondering . . . wondering if you would be brave. My brother was never very brave, Olivier.*
That's it, that's enough. You look at the bag between your feet for a while. Then you look up at me. I crook my finger at you: come closer. You move your face toward mine and I kiss you very gently on your golden cheek.
*I'm going to stop being your teacher now. Are you hungry?*
*No. I like it when you're my teacher.*
And that, I suppose, says everything.

It's not true that my parents live in Saanich, so this is where it gets tricky. Let's do it this way: my brother's waiting for us at the ferry terminal and you close up the car, sit in the back pretending not to be there. Which is fine. I ask him things: girlfriend? job? Mom, Dad, home? He's friendly. This might happen to you: you might learn to be friendly before you're thirty. He asks me: Edmund? job? Montreal? I'm glad to see him. He looks strong, golden as you are, but his hair is dark and his eyes are puppy-dog brown. They always used to cry too easily. Maybe yours did too, once, until you built yourself a box.
The greatest gift you could ever give me would be to let me see you cry.
We run out of things to say, and drive along in silence. *Oliver,* I ask, *what are those trees with the peeling red bark and the green inside?*
You say, *I don't know,* and he says, *I don't know.*

## Operculum

At home, my mother and father are in the kitchen making dinner: salmon and baked potatoes. My father wipes his hand quickly and uncomfortably on a dishtowel and extends it briskly to shake yours. He pronounces your name *o liv ee-ur*. My mother bustles you to your room as my father kisses me. My brother disappears and then what? I'm running out of ideas here, and this time . . . with the others I knew what I wanted to get to, but here I'm not sure. I've just come for a couple of days and then I'm going back to my life without you. Even in my mind I can't have more than a snatched moment of you. Why is that?

Let's have dinner. I suspect you don't like fish, and sure enough, you pick at your food. I sit next to you, maybe thinking that I have to look after you. I want to lean over and say warm jokes in your ear, so we can smile together and be friends, but I don't know what to say. My father looks disapprovingly at the cap you're wearing at the table. This is a reason to whisper to you. You take it off and your buckwheat-honey hair is smooth against your head, flying out at the long ends.

This is crucial. At this moment you will understand that you're afraid of my father. And my mother? I'm not sure who my mother is in this story, but you have your own mother, and don't need mine. And my brother? He's sitting across from you and neither of you speaks. My brother is trying to forget what it's like to be sixteen, and have your fuck-ups vague and potential, as opposed to done and irreversible.

Do I realize, here at the table, looking around, that bringing you here was wrong? That I've deceived you, and them, and that telling myself these stories is a waste of my love? You're gone, Olivier. What I really want to know is whether you have stories in your mind too, but I won't ever know that. What I want is not you, but a second chance. And what's done is done. Things can happen in five weeks that can't happen in life. The problem is that my brother is in my life. I'm not making him up.

If my parents lived anywhere together, if they lived in Saanich and we sat at the dinner table with them, there would be nothing that any of us could say that would make things right. Nothing, at least, that I can think of. There are too many things that would need to be real first, and I don't even know if anything you ever wrote to me was true.

Here's something I could do: I could take you to the Royal British Columbia Museum and show you the Haida masks of Gagiit. I could tell you how Gagiit lured those who had almost drowned into the woods to take away their souls, leaving them to wander the beaches alone eating raw shellfish with their hands. *That's disgusting,* you'd say. I'd show you my favourite mask, the one with the sea urchin spines sewing Gagiit's lips. *My brother almost drowned once, I tell you, when we were small. I tried to save him but he tried to drown me too, and then my dad noticed, and rescued us. Our great-great-grandmother was a Haida Indian. You can see it in Oliver in the summertime; the sun comes out and he turns the colour of the red-brown bark on those peeling trees we saw.*

*Me too,* you say.

*Yes, you look like you'd tan pretty dark.*

*No, I mean, I almost drowned when I was a kid.*

*Oh yeah?* And, even as I'm imagining it, this catches me by surprise.

*Yeah. Here, on Vancouver Island, jumping off the rocks into the sea. I knocked my head on something and they had to take me to the hospital with a . . . commotion cérébrale.*

*A concussion.*

*Yeah. I never asked who pulled me out of the water. I always thought it was probably my dad.*

We could go downstairs to the Natural History exhibit . .

. do you even like museums? But surely you like things like bugs and rocks and trees. We could see the tree there, the peeling tree ... if I could remember the name I could picture us looking at the description lit in front of the gloomy glass.

Here's something I remember. I'd show you my favourite thing, my favourite tiny thing in any museum anywhere: I'd take you back up to the First Nations gallery, past Gagiit once again. I'd take you into the back where they show all the things they use to make masks, and I'd show you an operculum, one of the rough morsels attached to the wall with threads so people won't take them away. I'd point at a white translucent one for you to touch. *What is it?* you'd ask.

And I'd say:

*It's the plate that covers the opening at the mouth of a shell.*

So I go right back to Schwartz Bay and get on the ferry and maybe I take you with me, but maybe there's no you any more. I see killer whales on the way back, though, the first whales I've ever seen in real life. I'm leaning over the railing, watching the black water pour by in white ripples, and a voice comes over the loudspeaker and everyone rushes to where I am. There are black arcs leaping out of the water out there, four six eight, and then they throw their white bellies up to the sun, up to us, I swear they're rolling over one another's backs as though they love each other. Two break free and chase our boat, firing themselves in black lace-edge patterns into the water we're rumbling. And there's your golden-brown face just above my ear, and the nearness of your glowing bones, the whisper of healed flesh on your forearm and I look up into your silver eyes like stars that are running for the finish line and your voice comes out all breath and as true as it would be if you were real and says *I've never seen anything so fucking cool.*

Or maybe. . . .

And in the end, this is just as likely. . . .

Maybe you're still at the dining table with my mother and my father and my brother, and when my mother sees that you won't eat the salmon she offers you a peanut butter sandwich, and my brother asks my father the name of those trees with the green wood and the red peeling bark, and my father says, *Arbutus trees, the only evergreen deciduous in the world* . . . and I sail off to Tsawwassen still not sure that I'll never see you cry, still not minding that you probably told me lies, and still waiting for a letter to hit the floor, whether or not I'm there and awake to hear it.

ACKNOWLEDGMENTS

Many of these pieces, or earlier versions of them, have been previously published:

"Bottle Episode" in *She Writes: Love, Spaghetti and Other Stories by Youngish Women* (Second Story Press) and *side/lines: A New Canadian Poetics* (Insomniac Press); "Aerugo" in *Grain*; "Universal Recipients" in *You and Your Bright Ideas: New Montreal Writing* (Véhicule Press); "Just Ahead of Us in Line" in *Room of One's Own*; "What Might Have Been Rain" in *Index*; and "Wall of Weeds" in *subTerrain*.

"Begin and End Frequently," "It Tastes Sweet," and "What Might Have Been Rain" were originally published in *What Might Have Been Rain: Short Stories* (1998). Much gratitude and love to Andy Brown of Conundrum Press.

"Aerugo" was the first-prize winner in *Grain*'s 1999 Short Grain Postcard Story Contest. "Operculum" was a runner-up in Anvil Press' International 3-Day Novel Contest (1998).

Many thanks to my editors, both formal and informal, without whom these pieces would have remained in various stages of much greater disarray: Blaine Kyllo and Brian Lam; Anne Fleming, my Banff Wired Writing Studio mentor; Taien Ng-Chan, Liane Keightley, Francesca LoDico, and Meg Sircom; and Catherine Bush and the members of her 1998-99 Concordia Prose Workshop.

Special thanks to Corey Frost, who not only made many of these stories better, but was there when some of them happened.

Thanks to the Canada Council for the Arts and the Conseil des arts et des lettres du Québec for funding my life during the final stages of the editing of this manuscript.

And finally, thank you to Arsenal Pulp Press.